ROD   Rodriguez Julia,
           Edgardo, 1946-

       The renunciation.

$18.00   505460205484335

DATE			

THE RENUNCIATION

THE RENUNCIATION

by Edgardo Rodríguez Juliá

A NOVEL

➤◄

Translated from the Spanish
by Andrew Hurley

Four Walls Eight Windows New York/London
UNESCO Publishing Paris

UNESCO COLLECTION OF REPRESENTATIVE WORKS
La renuncia del héroe Baltasar © 1972, 1986 by Edgardo Rodríguez Juliá
Translation © UNESCO 1997

Published in the United States by
Four Walls Eight Windows
39 West 14th Street
New York, NY 10011

U.K. offices:
Four Walls Eight Windows/Turnaround Distribution
Unit 3 Olympia Trading Estate
Coburg Road, Wood Green
London N22 6TZ

Library of Congress Cataloging-in-Publication Data:
Rodríguez Juliá, Edgardo, 1948–   [Renuncia del héroe Baltasar, English] The renucioation: a novel/by Edgardo Rodríguez Juliá; translated from the Spanish by Andrew Hurley. p. cm. ISBN 1-56858-057-6.—ISBN 9231031627 (UNESCO)
I. Hurley, Andrew. II. Title. PQ7440.R595R413 1997 863—dc21   97-23728 CIP

UNESCO ISBN 92-3-103162-7
10 9 8 7 6 5 4 3 2 1

Printed in the United States

Text design by Ink, Inc.

The translator would like to thank the University of Puerto Rico, College of Humanities, for the release time granted from teaching duties for the translation of this work.

LECTURE I

In Chapters X and XI of my book *A History and Guide to San Juan*, I included a brief biographical sketch of the fascinating and distinguished figure Baltasar Montañez. Tonight I would like to return—upon the invitation of this learned institution, and at the flattering request of my dear friend Eduardo Martínez Archilla, secretary of the Section on Historical Studies—to a consideration of that enigmatic hero of eighteenth-century Puerto Rico who has such profound historical significance for us today. For although Baltasar Montañez is indeed an enigma, and as such makes a claim upon our attention, our historical conscience, and our investigations, I believe that when we more fully understand this figure that passes across our history like some ominous dark cloud, he will have much to say to us, from the distance of centuries, about our common human condition.

I have said that Baltasar Montañez is a figure of profound historical significance, but before I plunge into the murky waters of that far-off eighteenth century of our land, I must make clear what I mean by that assertion:

Baltasar Montañez did not alter history or bring about profound change in it. If we compare him with his father, Ramón Montañez—that courageous leader of the Negro uprising of 1734—the life of the son can hardly be considered significant at all; his light hardly shines outside that minor history that Unamuno called "intrahistory." Why, then, do I speak of the historical significance of this man?

Baltasar is less important to History itself, with a capital *H*, than to the understanding of what the French call *la condition humaine.* It should not surprise us that the great poet of the human condition, our own Alejandro Juliá Marín, took Baltasar as the inspiration for his finest prose poems. Baltasar Montañez is, then, on the one hand a mere small historical fact, yet he stands as testimony to the darkest, most obscure, most veiled aspects of human nature. He is both history with a profound human meaning and dimension, and an eloquent witness to ourselves. I do not mean to suggest by this that there are historical figures without that particular human meaning and dimension; far from it—I believe that if we have any notion at all of what has generally been called human nature, it is because History, like a mirror, holds up to us, for our contemplation, an image of ourselves. But I do wish to emphasize that in History we sometimes find figures of rather insignificant-appearing stature who yet have great human dimensions and to suggest to you that those figures conspire as much as the larger ones—sometimes, perhaps, even more effectively—to forge or confirm that image that we have of ourselves. Baltasar Montañez is one of those figures. His place, his niche, lies somewhere between History with a capital *H* and intrahistory, between the noisiness of the great historical event and the whisper of lives that have gone untold. His place lies in that twilight the German Romantic poet Kleisthoffen called the "equivocal region of myth and legend." For the historian, that is the most difficult region to explore, for it requires the science of research, but also the magic of imagination.

->-<-

Baltasar Montañez's first renunciation took place on the afternoon of June 1, 1753, the day of his marriage to Josefina Prats, the daughter of don Tomás Prats, the secretary of state. What was it that Baltasar renounced? In the first place, he renounced his own race, his own people. A black man, after all, was marrying the daughter of the island's highest colonial dignitary. That meant that this *déclassé*, this upstart, this intruder would have to renounce his blackness, the culture of the shanties—which was a mixture of all the many ancient cultures of the west coast of Africa that had been transplanted to the New World—and adopt the social, cultural, and religious forms of the white upper-crust "society" of colonial Puerto Rico of the eighteenth century.

He also renounced his father's memory, and the revolutionary struggle that Ramón Montañez, captain and standard-bearer of the first and fiercest Negro uprising of that convulsed century, had fought and died for. In fact, as I made clear in my previous article on Baltasar, the marriage between the son of the rebel general (for so Ramón Montañez would have been called had his struggle been "on the right side") and the daughter of the secretary of state was intended specifically to have a calming effect on the revolutionary energies that that general had so bravely unleashed. The marriage was intended to offer up a sort of fairy-tale figure which would tranquilize, which would sedate, which would *dope,* black indignation. Baltasar Montañez would create in the black population the false illusion of freedom and social mobility. The intention was to slow or stop the revolutionary impulse by setting up the figure of a popular hero who would reconcile the two opposed classes. Baltasar Montañez became a traitor to his father's cause, for he allowed himself to be used to confuse his people, to relieve social stresses, which had they continued would have meant either the abolition of slavery or the overthrow of the colonial government. The hero of the celebrations of the feast of St. Peter and St. Paul in 1753, the winner and survivor of those literally breakneck horse races down the steep, narrow cobblestone streets of colonial San Juan, was now rebelling against his own father's ashes.

The colonial authorities did everything in their power, and they had a great deal of power, to spin an aura of myth and magic around Baltasar. They not only erected a monument on the site of the miracle attributed to his person, they attempted to make of him a charismatic figure who could gain the confidence of his people. The portrait of

Baltasar painted by Juan Espinosa in 1754 shows a handsome young black man dressed in the viceregal uniform of the Order of Calatrava and bearing the gold sword of the inquisitorial Order of the Indies. So within a year the humble cane cutter had been transformed into a high-ranking colonial official, doubly endowed with the trappings of his destined office: the vestments of those who had fought and conquered the Moor in that *other* noble Christian crusade and the sword of those who had tamed the savage Caliban of the Caribbean. There can be no doubt today, I believe, that the incident of the horse plunging over the wall at the bottom of Cristo Street during the races of the 1753 *fiestas* was not a miracle, but only a "miracle," in ironic quotation marks—a staged miracle, that is, and one staged precisely in order to capture the popular imagination. In support of this assertion, I ask you to consider a dispatch from Bishop José Larra—that *eminence grise* of eighteenth-century island politics—to Secretary of State don Tomás Prats:

> And Your Excellency will cry *Save him! Save him, Santo Cristo de la Salud!* and with that cry to our Savior who raised Lazarus from the dead and made the blind to see and the lame to walk, the hearts of those in the streets will be inflamed with pious emotion, and the cry of *Miracle!* will be heard from some voice in the crowd, and all of this *ad majorem Dei gloriam.* The

rider—who shall have received orders from the council to that effect—will pull up his mount, a magnificent animal according to the testimony of the grooms and hostlers of my stables, at the very verge of the precipice. All of this will produce a great confusion, and the happiness of the good parishioners whom I am honored to lead along the path to eternal salvation will attribute to the Divine hand that which in truth has human cause. It is essential to plant in the people's hearts a pious reverence for this miracle which by men has been manifested, yet which is justified by God our Heavenly Father as ministering to the tranquility and peace of His beloved children.

Although the top of this dispatch is somewhat mutilated and the bishop's first words lost, the drift is clear: as the young rider begins to come dangerously close to the wall at the bottom of the street and the horse threatens to plunge over the precipice to its, and its rider's, death, Secretary of State Prats will cry out for a miracle; when the horse, under the skilled hand of Baltasar, stops inches from the wall, someone in the crowd—a person in the pay of the bishop—will cry out the word *Miracle!* Thus the first part of the legend, the myth of the heroic Baltasar touched by miracle, will begin to take shape.

Let me call your attention to Bishop Larra's reference to those "orders from the council" received by Baltasar.

This confirms our suspicion not only that Baltasar knew about the plot from the outset, but that the "miracle" associated with him was staged with his consent and collaboration. It is important to stress this point because in some of his later writings Baltasar will speak about the miracle as though fully convinced of its divine nature.

After his marriage to Josefina Prats, the handsome young hero paid a visit or visits to the colonies of Negroes that had established themselves on the sugar cane plantations of the north coast. Like some Prometheus intending to steal fire from the colonial gods, he announced that his presence in the Fortress of Santa Catalina, the Palace of State, promised great good for his people. Thus the traitor to the revolution set in motion by Ramón Montañez attempted to create an image of himself as benefactor, a man who would lighten the Negroes' yoke of slavery. In other words, this entire maneuver was an attempt to put into practice what today we would call a policy of reform. The entire charade was directed by Bishop Larra, and was aimed at calming the aroused spirit of the black population of the island. Baltasar was Larra's puppet, an emancipated slave who was gestating—behind the careful disguise that always characterized him—the betrayal and oppression of his own people.

Bishop Larra's secretary speaks of the dark hopes for Baltasar in his *Crónica de lo sucedido bajo el obispado del muy insigne y santísimo su Excelencia Don José Larra de*

Villaespesa, or "Chronicle of the Events which Occurred During the Rule of the Most Distinguished and Holy Bishop his Excellency don José Larra de Villaespesa":

Of great benefit for the good health of the civil government of this city has been the most holy marriage contracted between Baltasar Montañez and doña Josefina Prats. Since the moment the most reverend Bishop Larra blessed this union under the holy sacrament of matrimony, calm has returned to the shepherd's most beloved flock. The primitive and idolatrous band of Negroes that had attempted to violate all that is beloved by Nature and sanctioned by God our Heavenly Father has now entered into the jaws to which its own condition had consigned it. This humble scribe now so briefly and crudely describing these scenes has witnessed with his own eyes how the man named Baltasar Montañez has carried himself with great signs of respect through the populations most convulsed by the erstwhile Luciferian rebellions. The rabble bows down before this puppet, this most plausible hero, and imagines that it sees in him its hopes for realizing its anomalous and diabolic desire to break its chains, and thereby violate the law set down by the God of Heaven. This man named Baltasar plays to utmost perfection the role of peacemaker between the two races that inhabit this small and beautiful island, and is restoring to firm foundations the hegemony of Christianity over heresy. This man has given some proof of his gifts for statecraft, and this I am able to declare because he encourages the heretical, wicked hopes of freedom in the Negroes while at the same time holding firmly in check their concupiscent impulses, proclaiming himself a prefiguration of the realization of their dreams and the worthy guarantor of those aspirations. With skilled and expert deceit he diverts diabolic violence with futile hopes, while he keeps a firm rein on the stampeding horse that is his race. Although I fear he is not a man who can long leave our prudence free of misgivings, his never-relinquished mask in his dealings with the mob of his people is certain to reap for his own low self all the pleasures that power has to offer, and that fact sets us in the very advantageous position of making an agreement between his profit and our own natural and privileged condition. His well-maintained pose as emancipator suits him, but also suits—by reason of the natural order, not subtle political intrigue—our own divinely sanctified Monarchy.

Bishop Larra's secretary points out the sweet political fruits harvested with the marriage of Baltasar and Josefina. And indeed, the revolutionary impulses of the blacks were checked by that social and political fantasy conceived by

Bishop Larra. The marriage acted as a kind of narcotic on the black population of the island, drugging the conscience as well as the consciousness of the slaves. The attempt to remove the necessity of revolution was apparently successful; the Negro masses were hoodwinked by the illusion of freedom. The calming effect had been achieved.

But let us go back a few steps and delve a little deeper into the circumstances that surrounded that curious marriage. In the first place, sufficient documentary evidence is in our possession to prove that in fact Secretary of State Prats refused to allow his daughter to be sacrificed to such an end, and refused with even more horror to give his permission for his child to be thrown to this black Moloch. Since my previous article, I have discovered evidence of a bitter exchange of letters between Bishop Larra and Secretary Prats. Prats's refusal led to his arrest and imprisonment, but he was not actually removed from office until after the wedding. With one exception, all the chronicles of the time report Prats's presence at his daughter's wedding. Yet when we look into the matter a bit further we begin to suspect that Secretary Prats was, at the hour of his daughter's nuptials, under house arrest. That June 1 of the year 1753 hides a secret behind the frenzied music of the celebrating Negroes and the complications of colonial protocol: the kidnapping and sequestration of the entire Prats family. Larra's collaborator in the Cristo Street miracle refused to offer the hand and the virginity of his beautiful daughter as the means of achieving the political ends that Bishop Larra sought, the calming of the black populace. Thus, tonight I am reconsidering the opinions which I expressed in my *History and Guide to San Juan.* There, I pointed to Secretary Prats as the author, so to speak, of the marriage. Today I wish to correct that assessment of the incident to establish, in the light of my latest findings, that Bishop Larra was in fact the genius behind the plan.

Yet this does not explain why I subscribed to such a mistaken idea of the historical circumstances for so long. Let us see why I might have: The document that led me to uphold the mistaken thesis is the bombastically titled *Crónica oficial de los muy dignos Secretarios del Obispo Don José Larra en torno al muy apoteósico matrimonio de Don Baltasar Montañez y Doña Josefina Prats,* or "The Official Report Prepared by the Most Worthy Secretaries to Bishop don José Larra in Order to Chronicle the Magnificent Wedding of don Baltasar Montañez to doña Josefina Prats." Who were these most worthy secretaries? One of them was named don Ramón García Oviedo, but in keeping with the customs of the time, he used the somewhat imposing pseudonym John of Golgotha. The other, don Alonso Bustamante y Morales, received the curious *"purificante,"* or "purifying appellation," as these pseudonyms were called, of Brother of the Skull. The first time I read the reports that these two men had written of the nuptials, I overlooked one extremely significant detail. In one of

the chronicles, to call it by the name they themselves gave
their reports, specifically the chronicle of don Alonso Bustamante y Morales, there is a long list of the dignitaries present at the wedding. Striking for its absence—and I now see
that I was almost infinitely dull witted in not noticing this
from the beginning—is the name of Secretary of State
Prats. According to the handwritten manuscript now in
the collection of the Carnegie Library in San Juan, this
chronicle was written on June 10, 1753. On July 22 of that
same year another report, or chronicle, was written, this
time by don Ramón García Oviedo. In this latter report
there is an almost obsessive insistence on Prats's presence
on what was designated the "nuptial balcony of La Fort-
aleza," the governor's palace. The good spirits and broad
smile of the secretary are mentioned, and much is made of
his fatherly pride. Perhaps, though, this chronicle should
speak for itself:

> And on the balcony there also could be seen lending
> distinction to the event with his most dignified and
> erect mien, the most excellent Secretary of State Prats,
> and this brilliant island luminary followed every detail
> of the ceremony with all the remarkable satisfaction of
> the proud and happy father who knows that he has led
> his beloved child always down the paths of righteous-
> ness and holiness. There he stood in all the excellence
> of his person, smiling and in sober yet splendid ele-

gance, and all this raised to the supreme heights of splendorous magnificence in covering his handsome person with the extremely rich and impressive uniform of the Order of St. Jerome of the Colonies. Brightest jewel of island authority! There he shed his light on all the generations to come! This great gentleman of the Indies!

The first time I examined these documents, as I say, the first report I read was this one I have just quoted to you—a report, I remind you, written six weeks *after* the wedding. So when I read the document dated June 10, that is, the document which had been written only a few days after the event, probably with the intention of publication in the *Island Gazette*,[1] I overlooked, clumsy researcher that I am, its omission of the name of Secretary of State Prats. Considerable time passed before I went back, this time equipped, metaphorically at least, with a magnifying glass, to examine the documents again. And what to my amazement did I discover? In addition to the omission I have already mentioned in the chronicle of June 10, the main text of the July 22 document *also* did not contain any mention of the Secretary of State—Prats's presence was detailed in

1. The *Gaceta Oficial Insular* was, more than a newspaper, the official register of governmental decrees and announcements. Publication of the June 10 chronicle would have made that document the *official* report of the nuptials. Little wonder it was never published.

marginalia, later additions to the report. It was from these marginalia that I took the lines I have just quoted to you.

But surprise followed upon surprise. The handwriting of the marginalia is completely different from the handwriting of the text. It is obvious, then, that the marginalia were not written by don Ramón García Oviedo. To put it less than elegantly, something was fishy here.

I returned to the chronicle written by don Alonso Bustamante, which was the first report written on the wedding. Dated June 10, as I have said, it stands in closest proximity to the event. Though don Alonso was probably well aware of Prats' fate, he seems to have tried to gloss over the thorny matter by simply omitting any reference to the father of the bride. It is clear that Bishop Larra was beside himself when he read this first report. Its omission of Prats's name is tantamount to an accusatory finger. (If I was not struck by the absence of any mention of Prats it was because I had first read the altered report of July 22.) Bishop Larra immediately wrote the following note to the person who was to make the alteration to the second chronicle:

It is with singular surprise that we have become aware of the noxious effect to the health of the body politic that may be entailed by the formal report on that state wedding which has been a subject dear to our recent concern. The reason for this is that in the chronicle submitted as testimony of the event by the Brother of the Skull, one cannot but note the absence of all mention of Secretary of State Prats. I acknowledge my own unpardonable distraction from the necessities of governance in not issuing clear and particular orders regarding such a serious matter; but at any rate, the person guilty for the omission from the record shall be justly punished, since as an officer of the Crown he should clearly have been more sensible of the grave necessities of the Crown in such a tender matter. The only consolation which at this late date we may offer ourselves is that our own private secretary and consular scribe for all episcopal protocols, the most excellent don Ramón García Oviedo, has begun a new report on that eminent event. And in this latest chronicle, the white lie[2]—which by Divine will may be the only remedy for this most serious breach—shall be equivalent to the truth, for such a white lie is the only recourse which may maintain us in conditions of peace, and peace is the only end sought by God the all-merciful. . . .

To whom was this note sent? No document supports the assertion that I am about to make, but I believe that the letter was sent to Baltasar Montañez. We must note that Bishop Larra acknowledges his responsibility for the omission, in

2. In Spanish, "*mentira piadosa*," a "pious" or "merciful" lie, one spoken in order to do good or avoid doing harm, one spoken with divine sanction for the good results thereby produced. It is an "ends justify the means" lie.

effect apologizing, and promises that the chronicler will be chastened, at the least. It would only be before Baltasar Montañez, as the foundation stone of Larra's proslavery and procolonial policies, that the terrible and powerful Bishop Larra would have eaten such mock humble pie.

But my magnifying glass continued to bring out details and to clear up mysteries: I was in fact able to attribute to Baltasar Montañez the marginalia added to Oviedo's chronicle. The handwriting of these additions corresponds to that found on several of Baltasar's manuscripts, which I have in my possession. The style is Baltasar's: verbose, rhetorical, slightly pompous, the result of a perhaps over-rapid cultural assimilation. We should recall in this regard that Baltasar was a man of very little learning before he married doña Josefina. His great intelligence—one might almost call it true genius—allowed him to acquire, within a very few years, tremendous culture, but this legacy, untried by the slow fire of years of tempering, was in truth a pathetic caricature of erudition. Baltasar parodied, unwittingly of course, the hyperbolic style of the Spanish intellectuals of the eighteenth century. That style which Helfeld has called "the twilight of the baroque" became, in the uncertain hands of Baltasar, an exaggeration of an exaggeration. Of course it is not simply the rococo style that makes his prose so remarkable and distinctive; we also see prefigured in the marginalia the hysterical style of Baltasar's *Crónica de la muy ingeniosa concepción de una arquitectura militar que consiste en la disposición de la Naturaleza en un paisaje mortal* ("A Chronicle of a Most Ingenious Plan for a Military Architecture Consisting of the Disposition of Nature in a Mortal Landscape"), which I will discuss in my second and third lectures. Of course it is not strictly speaking the hysteria of a visionary that we see in the marginalia: such exclamatory glorification no doubt springs from resentment at the spectacle of this "brightest jewel of island authority" who refused to see his daughter married to a black man. Fury at the absence of his father-in-law from the wedding, outrage and resentment stemming from the humiliating falsification of Prats's presence at the nuptials, reach their culmination in these violent, pain-filled words: "There he shed his light on all the generations to come! This great gentleman of the Indies!"

That trope "brightest jewel of island authority" is very like Baltasar. The following quotation is Baltasar Montañez as he tells how he met the architect Juan Espinosa: "In 1754 not one architect lived on the island. It was for that reason that the Secretary of State Prats, whose benevolence has been the brightest jewel of island authority, sent for an architect, don Juan Espinosa...." We know today that the construction of the chapel dedicated to that Christ who raised Lazarus from the dead and made the blind see and the lame walk, the chapel at the foot of the steep hill of Cristo Street, could not have been ordered by Tomás Prats, for in 1754 he was in prison, stripped of his important position. Why would Baltasar construct this immense fiction? The answer is clear: For his own legitimacy, and for his own pride as well, he needed the presence and acceptance of don Tomás. Hurt and rejected, Baltasar and his diabolic pride must have erected a sort of myth, a fiction according to which Prats wished to honor the memory of the miraculous black man. Today we can state, without fear of error, that the construction of the famous chapel was carried out by order of Bishop Larra.

In July of 1753 there appeared the chronicle written by Oviedo, the Bishop's secretary, with the marginalia by Baltasar. It received Bishop Larra's blessing. The white lie, the holy lie, is forged: Tomás Prats approved the marriage of his daughter to the Negro Baltasar. It was necessary that the people know the "official line" on this thorny matter. Everyone, from that moment on, was to picture to him- or herself Secretary Prats's pleased smile, his presence on the sad nuptial balcony of the governor's palace.

Many colonial officials and dignitaries withheld their approval of Baltasar and Larra's fiction. In a letter sent to the secretary of judicial affairs of the city of San Juan Bautista (the district attorney, we might call him today), Bishop Larra demanded the immediate arrest and trial of don Alonso Bustamante. We already know what he was to be charged with: refusing to include in the list of functionaries attending the wedding the name of a man who at the time of the base event was imprisoned in some dark, wet cell in the prison of San Felipe del Morro, nursing, with the memory of the dewy and angelic beauty of his daughter, his desperation. Don Alonso was imprisoned on July 24, 1753, and what became of him afterward is still a dark mystery to us. These are the words of Bishop Larra to the secretary of judicial affairs:

> The immediate arrest, trial, and conviction of His Majesty's subject don Alonso Bustamante will be of very great advantage to the peace and tranquility of this city. The aforementioned subject has made public, in the form of a handbill posted about the city's squares, a libelous account which by the falseness of its nature threatens the peace and tranquility of our beloved flock.

On that same date Bishop Larra wrote the following words in this book titled *Aforismos para la santa y verdadera educación del hombre del estado,* or "Aphorisms for the True and Holy Education of the Statesman":

> Inopportune truth is as noxious to the safety and security of States as is the fire of Mars. There are no more dangerously disposed men than those who would put truth above the necessities of the Universal Good. Truth without piety or mercy—that is, that which does not take into consideration the passing weak nature of men and of their condition—is as repugnant as the poison of

those political men who believe in deceit—*o cave dolum!*—as the only means of governing. Thus it is that God, in His infinite wisdom, has given us the highly praiseworthy instrument of the calming "white lie," the pious, well-intended, and compassionate untruth-become-sweet-truth, whose source lies not in the swollen pride of those impious men who believe themselves worthy of beatification for their purity, which in truth is a quality that hobbles the talent that God has given men for their survival, but lies rather in the recognition of our common fallen nature, which has plunged us into sin, and which tends more toward pleasurable passion than unsullied truth. A white lie pales further yet before the spectacle of our human condition. To tell a white lie is to tailor divine truth to human stature. Truth is but a dark reflection through man's falsehoods. Without falsehood, truth would be a mute and obscure virgin lost in the silence of a terrifying universe.

We do not know the fate of the chronicler García Oviedo, but well we might suppose that it was similar to that of don Alonso Bustamante. In August of 1753, Bishop Larra had a new secretary, don Rodrigo Pérez de Tudela, whose testimony regarding the pacification attendant on Baltasar's marriage we have already heard.

Let us look once again at the duel between Bishop Larra and Secretary of State Prats as it is recorded in those documents that still exist. I am about to read you a missive, dated March 23, 1753, in which Bishop Larra attempts to convince don Tomás Prats of the political desirability of giving his daughter's hand in marriage to Baltasar. These are Bishop Larra's words:

> Obliged by these troubled times to seek the recourse of begging you, my very dear and esteemed and most worthy friend, to agree to the magnificent marriage of your most delicate and beloved daughter Josefina to the free citizen Baltasar Montañez, and that, for most pressing reasons of state, I would cite certain vexatious and distressing circumstances which lead me to the decided assurance that such a union would be the greatest possible guaranty of peace and tranquility for the years to come.
>
> A union between Baltasar and Josefina—a woman blessed by the roses that the angels from heaven scattered over these most harsh and difficult tropics— would serve to placate the storms of violence which, for the last five decades of Our Lord Jesus Christ, since the diabolic and most barbarous rebellion of that satanic Ramón Montañez, have been a scourge to the good order of our blessed insular Monarchy. The marriage would serve to inseminate a most powerful fantasy in the Negro masses, who in equal parts deluded and deluding would thereby be the more profoundly

tamed. For them, what magnificent victory, to see one of their own raised into the high spheres of the universe by Our Heavenly Father! Our subtle reasoning in the cause of good government gives us to understand that this marriage would bring about in the dusky ranks of the Negro masses that state of euphoric concupiscence which so dulls and stupefies the inferior races, and causes them to become unconscious of the baseness of their condition. We would celebrate these nuptials with the most splendid celebrations, in which the Negro masses would squander, in lustful diversions, in the alcohol distilled from sugar cane that they call *angelito,* and in the dance they call I believe *macumbe,* if I have it right, their impulse toward revolution. And thus these poor creatures of the Lord would return to the path of goodness, blinded by the triumph which in truth signifies for them terrible defeat, their uncouth heads filled with a fantasy combining pleasure and vengeance, while they themselves are but the frail embers of a fire now virtually extinguished. But all of these loud festivities before mentioned should be restrained and most carefully overseen by a large concentration of *carabineros* that we shall have stationed in the plaza and at the Palace of State. What was once feared rebellion will be converted into drunken and savage riot; that Machiavellian fire whose devouring flames recall the farts of the satanic monk named Luther, and which threatened the Lord's house, will be well averted by this sweet marriage that I advise, a marriage which will stand as an emblem of the cordial union between the two races that inhabit this realm.

Your excellency must not dwell overmuch upon the disposition and appearance of Baltasar Montañez. Think of him as but that young man of good Negro stock that your excellency and I your humble servant together bore to great heroism with the most holy miracle that occurred during the last festival of St. Peter and St. Paul. The marriage with your most worthy daughter would be the apex of that high mount up whose slopes we carried Baltasar Montañez for the political good of our island and the welfare of our beloved people. Baltasar shows good, spirited, and truly wondrous disposition to undertake the utter destruction of the demonic work of his father. He is a well-pleased young man who offers his high heart to the most holy work of deceiving his inferior beings, and he is provided with a most cynical mind, which is repugnant to us even within the absolute good that is presented us to do. Once as I was conversing with this most opportune traitor, he praised our omnipotent monarchy, but it is not for that that his state rises above that of the serpent that crawls in obscure silence, and that stings with surprise, or the vulture, which like that intriguing Aragonese Antonio

Pérez, secretary to Philip II and infamous for his machinations against the state, hovers in readiness to sate himself upon carrion, and I was most astonished to hear him give voice to the following words: "I, most faithful servant, hate my people. And that, as the issue of the intense love that I felt for my father. When my father was killed, I was present for that lesson. It was when my father was felled on the boulders of the surf-beaten coast; his humors were spilled onto the rocks while the mass of Negroes stood there stock-still, dark, impassive, silent, without a word of protest. I alone cried out, and I ran to my father's body. But the strong soldiers restrained me. And my spirit cried like my mother's. It was upon that day and with that deed that I determined within myself to bury beneath the face of the earth, in the clay, the face of my hated brethren. And so I bear within my entrails the desire to hate what was most beloved by my dear father. In my remarkable betrayal I love him and I revenge his death, but I also sink into mute hatred and contempt. And all this pain because he held another man his enemy." Your excellency can see in these words the ingenuity of our Baltasar, and what is more, the desperate and hopeless spirit that is determined above all else to seek revenge for his father, revenge turned upon those who for their most holy meekness and timidity bore him to his final lesson. It is high genius that hates its own sable skin, and from that most diabolical emotion in him there issues fire for his own brethren, as he admits, though inoffensive roses for our most beloved monarchy.

I have already informed you, with canonical justification, that should this union come to pass, the ceremony of marriage only—the forms of that ceremony, I mean to say—would be performed, and that it would have no sacramental value whatsoever. In the eyes of our Maker your most beloved daughter would not be married to the most impious Baltasar Montañez. The exchange of vows would be of most farcical intention. Every liturgical gesture would be performed, and yet none of the divine and sacramental intentions would be observed. As soon as the period of carnival ended, your daughter would be freed from the presence of the Negro so abominable to her taste. And that son of the arrogant demon whose eyes spat out flames would begin his prolonged marriage to the shadows of the stone dungeon within the labyrinth of our Catholic and blessèd fortress San Felipe del Morro.

But these words still do not reveal Larra's true hidden intentions. Immediately after the wedding ceremony, which was celebrated in the Santa Catalina Palace on June 1, 1753, Baltasar thwarted Bishop Larra's subtle, secret trick, by kidnapping his fearful young wife. I say kidnapped because thus the action was understood by that equally fearful society that we find reflected in don Rafael Contreras' report:

> And after the appearance of the splendidly bedecked couple, the young bridegroom Baltasar Montañez addressed his Negro followers. From that ragged and pestiferous mob there issued a dense smell of the harsh stinging brandy known as *angelito,* and which unleashes every concupiscent humor in them.

(By official government decree, you see, leave had been given the blacks to dance in the streets; there were unlimited supplies of *angelito*—which is a fiendishly powerful beverage made with cane alcohol, coconut milk, and the fermented juice of pineapple. But let us return to the relation of those dreadful events:)

> The Negro Baltasar spoke to his people, and said that he would come down into the streets with his wife to celebrate the immense happiness that filled his heart to overflowing. Just at the moment that he was making this surprising announcement, I saw upon the face of Bishop Larra a most ironic smile, which meant, to the eyes and understanding of all those there assembled who could read it, that Baltasar had taken the first piece in that most delicate chess game that is the preservation of power. And I state these things in this

frank and forthright manner because the intentions of
Bishop Larra for the hours and days succeeding the
holy nuptials were very well known throughout all the
spheres of power on the island. His excellency Bishop
Larra had intended to arrest and imprison the Negro
Baltasar Montañez after the much-desired and most
gratifying ceremony. But now, with the people's hero
celebrating with his own, that arrest was only possible
if the island were willing to pay the terrible price of a
most terrible, widespread, and bloody uprising.

Don Rafael, of course, was mistaken in his interpretation
of Bishop Larra's smile. It would have been absurd for Larra
to have imprisoned Baltasar just when Larra stood at the per-
fect juncture for achieving peace between the races. Under
that carefully deceitful smile, Larra cloaked the pact that he
had reached not with don Tomás Prats but with *Baltasar*—a
pact which provided that Baltasar, the hero of the Negro
masses, would carry the shy Josefina into the heart of the
black celebration. The words of the bishop's letter to Secretary of State Prats were filled with falsehood and deception.
He simply wished to put Secretary of State Prats's mind tem-
porarily at ease, as the secretary still wielded some influence
and commanded some sympathy among the colonial leadership. Indeed, Bishop Larra had led not just Prats but even
his closest collaborators to believe that he would imprison
Baltasar after the ceremony. By dissembling in that way, he

could deflect from himself any blame for the terrible debasement of sweet Josefina that followed the act. Of course on the other hand, everyone believed, as did don Rafael Contreras, that the price of Baltasar's arrest would be a rebellion of the drunken Negro masses. It was the subtle reasoning of Bishop Larra—like all confessors the finest of psychologists—that although Baltasar's imprisonment was incongruent with the aims for peace that the marriage pretended to further, aims which his collaborators had so zealously favored, these same collaborators would, out of fear of Baltasar and the consequences of that tremendous political gamble, wind up willing themselves to believe the story of Baltasar's imminent arrest. This desire to believe allowed the Bishop's true intentions to go unperceived. Everyone feared the sinister exchange of vows that would debase the most delicate flower of her race, yet desired to believe (indeed, did at last believe) that all power would devolve onto the idolatrous and sacrilegious Negro. And yet at the same time, they believed that this power might be curbed, through the intercession of Bishop Larra, once there existed the possibility of a great spilling of white blood. This psychological situation is outlined in a poem by Alejandro Juliá Marín titled "The Bishop Sows His Seeds":

They are possessed by a fear which all powers would
    persuade them to forget:
Horrible scenes of children murdered, women raped,

and men castrated follow one upon another, when there arrive with the dawn long caravans of black, shrouded wagons.

"It is like a river that we have unleashed into all its possible and infinite courses. And we, of such white skin, so alone, now victims of the sweat that flows down from the cane fields ..."

Then it is that they come to believe with religious fervor in the promise of force that Bishop Larra made them: "Baltasar will be imprisoned after the wedding takes place ... "

But how is it possible that Bishop Larra could agree to Josefina's humiliation in that way? We can imagine the indignation aroused among the white populace by the scene of that delicate adolescent woman, a girl almost, surrounded by a drunken, dancing mob of black men and women, and then dragged through streets that stank of the frenzied sweat of the *macumbreros,* as the dancers were known. There can be no doubt that Bishop Larra recognized in Baltasar's act a threat to his plan. It was Baltasar, after all, who decided that he would celebrate his nuptials by degrading and humiliating Josefina. It was he who had imposed that bizarre condition, and Bishop Larra had had to accept it in order to avert worse consequences yet, even while recognizing that in this condition lay a premature, and perhaps not the last, rebellion of the black instrument of his *raison d'etat.* Bishop

Larra considered the humiliation of young Josefina part of the price that had to be paid for the desired peace. Baltasar in turn recognized his own power, since he knew himself to be acting as the mediator between the two races, to be the site of the confluence of the mutual fear reflected in the eyes of both blacks and whites. Concerning this power that Baltasar recognized very early on in his career, Alejandro Juliá Marín has written the following meditation:

BALTASAR, THE MOST POWERFUL

There is a breast in which fear meets a smile. There power resides.

One gesture from Baltasar, and blood would splash across the plaza. But this young cynic thinks: More even than freedom, these people yearn for a dream, a fantasy that can fit their most secret desires.

(The girl-child—her white dress sullied—is frightened; she feels faint, and she cries when she feels the fiery scourging of her loins that the drums inflame. Beside her, Baltasar waves, gives a laugh that rumbles through the blue-black night, and squeezes the buttocks of dark María Asunción.)

But if he disappeared, if the dream-come-true turned invisible, the slaves would fight for their right to humiliate. And they would forget fear, and they would find many, though not so powerful.

And thus it is that Baltasar plays with the passions of men. That is how powerful he is.

Another piece of literary evidence bearing upon this premature triumph of Baltasar's over the designs of Bishop Larra may be found in Juliá Marín's play titled *The Hero Baltasar*. I will read you a brief extract from the scene in which Baltasar's will prevails over the "policy" of Bishop Larra:

ACT I, SCENE III

(After the wedding, in Larra's office.)

BALTASAR: My dear bishop, you would commit a grave error in refusing. Upon me depends the peace of this city . . .

BISHOP LARRA: *(Visibly angry.)* But what base pleasure do you derive from the humiliation of a woman already your legitimate wife?

BALTASAR: Please, your excellency—in my case there is no need to maintain that pretense.

BISHOP LARRA: *(Somewhat disturbed.)* Don't you see that the humiliation of Josefina would be a grave offense to the white population? And that *that* will mean most serious danger to our policy. . . .

BALTASAR: *Your* policy, my dear bishop.

BISHOP LARRA: As you wish; but remember that if the authorities' indignation grows too hot, you will be the first victim of our repression.

BALTASAR: The warning is unnecessary; but you in turn must understand that my fall from power would entail the bloodiest revolt this colony has yet seen. —Do you quail before the efficacy of your myth?

BISHOP LARRA: *(Recovering his serenity.)* Baltasar, Baltasar . . . Fly not so high, my friend; desire not to be master of so many lives. I know that pride goes with power—but proportion the first to the latter, my friend, or else. . . .

BALTASAR: Why try to hide your defeat? I am the most powerful man in all this land, and you, a man skilled in these arts, know that very well. Why am I the most powerful? I will tell you, then: I know the fear that you and your people feel each time that you look at a Negro, and I can unleash, not simply with my martyrdom but with a mere gesture, the dogs of the hunt for whites. My people are outside, there, drunk with happiness because one of the hated ones shall be humiliated. I shall not be the man to deny those beasts that pleasure. The number of Negroes in the city exceeds the population of whites by seven to one. Accept, my dear Bishop, that I *am* the master of lives, and properties as well. My people will humiliate the child that you and your people have thrown me like a bone to gnaw. You alone have sought this sacrifice.

BISHOP LARRA: *(Very agitated.)* Baltasar, Josefina cannot go down into that street. You must not dare carry out this terrible humiliation. It would bring on a situation untenable for the policy we have undertaken, and which is the country's only hope for peace. If the authorities turn against you, it can only

end, for your people and for my own as well, in most
terrible destruction.

BALTASAR: Those considerations do not move me.
Humiliating the whites does, exacting my revenge
upon the executioners of my father, and with them,
the Negroes that collaborated by their silence.

BISHOP LARRA: And how do you pretend to humiliate
your own people?

BALTASAR: By making possible for them that other
humiliation that is the only revenge that they can
conceive. The humiliation of the white man is the
only freedom the Negro seeks.

BISHOP LARRA: You belong to the most fearsome of
human species. Your logic is implacable, and you
have no compassion for human frailties.

BALTASAR: Quite right, my dear Bishop. I only play
with other men's passions. Men's lives are not for
me an occasion for compassion, but the opportunity
to exercise my talents. I thought that you too were
fond of intellectual games; I now see my error.

BISHOP LARRA: *(With impotent solemnity.)* You try my
patience, sir.

BALTASAR: You should rather look to trying out your
passions. If some mischance should befall me, the
Negroes *will* begin the destruction. I am master, fantasy, and culmination of their perverse desires! And
they will fight without mercy. . . . The debasement of

Josefina is a small price to pay for the life of your
entire race.

On June 7, 1753, there appeared in the streets of San
Juan the following anonymous notice:

Great sorrow and ignominy has been caused this city by
the spurious marriage of Josefina, the daughter of our
most worthy don Tomás Prats, even at this moment
imprisoned for having faithfully and honestly kept a
father's divine mission to watch over the life and honor
of his children. Sorrow of immense significance has
been caused this tender flower by having seen herself
bound, indeed manacled, by Bishop Larra's impious
reasonings of state and led to an infamous exchange of
wedding vows with, and equally infamous union to, a
Negro slave unworthy of marriage to the lightest woman
of his own low and degraded race. Ignominy has been
heaped upon ignominy by the imprisonment of don
Tomás Prats, a most honored and venerable gentleman
of this city, and most wounded father, whose sole and
unique crime has been to defend the irreproachable
purity and honor of his beloved daughter. This universal suffering of our people is owed solely to the most
Machiavellian reasonings of state of this Bishop of hell,
this Richelieu who is Satan's vicar, this monkish incar-
nation with the tongue of a viper and a great noise of

wind from the vent in his backside, who spreads the deceit and inflamed evil of those political men who sacrifice Christ to the Moloch of the State.

On June 12 there was yet another attack on Bishop Larra. His policy was weakening, his power base was eroding—the marriage had caused a wave of indignation in the white population; these anonymous attacks were aimed not so much at Baltasar as at the bishop, who was accused of the most impious and egregious Machiavellianism and branded a traitor to his race and religion. It was at that moment that there appeared the famous anonymous broadside titled "Notice of the Dragging through the Mud." This bill, posted throughout the city, reported Josefina's forced part in the black slaves' frenzied celebration of the wedding:

A piteous vision has filled my eyes with tears. The loveliest rose, the child Josefina, her senses overwhelmed by the frenzied music of this lewd and savage night black race, wandered through the streets on the arm of her criminal husband, her eyes wearied from the diabolical scenes to which she was witness, her clothing stained and sullied by the ignominious affront of those thousands of hands more simian than human. And beside the virginal white daisies of her hands, the black talons beating upon the leather skins of their drums. The child, ever theretofore protected by the most zealous decorum, the most discreet of upbringings, was dragged, for one long and torturous week, through those rivers of drunken and dancing Negroes that compose the most doleful populace of our beloved land. There was no corner, plaza, or doorway where one did not find the simians, felled by the drunkenness which, in concert with the Luciferian dull wittedness of Bishop Larra, had brought this good city to its current state of evil governance. And this was a thing which all might see with their own eyes, for at many corners of the city, great wagons were to be found, with huge barrels of that drink they call *angelito*, which is a crude and harsh ferment capable of stoking the fires of the bestiality of that race. Everywhere one found hundreds of Negroes milling about those enormous barrels, the bladders of Satan. And there was great disgust to see those beasts raise their cups, their hands trembling in frenzy and their bodies in violent commotion, to receive their portion of *angelito,* provided by the Machiavel Larra himself, thus imperilling the sweet peace of the Lord of Heaven and of Earth.

When will this unbridled madness pass? When will Satan cease to tempt the savagery of these base creatures? But to that great humiliation we must add vile insult, for as the child Josefina, in her sad pilgrimage through the mud, would approach two or more Negroes, they would shout *Here she comes! Here she comes!* and they would abandon their drums, their terrible *angelito,* call others' attention from the wagons, and hordes of them would make their way towards her in a mob, hurling filthy insults at her, and blasphemies in the tongues of Africa, and lewdly move their bodies before the most delicate eyes of this child, who was, nay still remains, the loveliest jewel of our island's authority.

But all that I have said before is but vain lament, if the authorities and good citizens of this city do not steel themselves to end this tyranny of the base simians, and to re-establish truth and reason as the divine guide for our Christian hegemony.

Who was the author of this broadside? In whose interest was it to inflame the indignation of the whites? Someone wished to begin a white revolt against the new masters of the city, that drunken mass of Negroes that threatened to destroy established order. Then the author must have been none other than Baltasar Montañez. Remember that last phrase, now becoming so familiar to us, from the next to last paragraph: "the loveliest jewel of our island authority." This phrase is virtually our hero's signature, our hero who plays hide-and-seek, as it were, between the lines of these documents. What perverse pleasure he must have derived from playing with fire beside a huge barrel of gunpowder! In toying with the possibility of unleashing a bloody confrontation between whites and blacks, Baltasar was attempting to avenge the death of his father. I say *toying* because in my view, power had a certain playful, ludic aspect for Baltasar, who was capable of inciting passions, setting the game in motion, and then standing back, with his cynical smile, like a god standing above vain human motives, to contemplate the futility of all effort.

Of course some of you will object that this stylistic proof is insufficient to convict, perhaps insufficient to indict—insufficient to attribute the "Notice of the Dragging through the Mud" to Baltasar. I will get a little ahead of myself, then, for those skeptics among you, and inform you of a fact that I believe is finally convincing: I have found, among Baltasar's unpublished papers, the draft of that notorious anonymous broadside. Except for a few parts omitted in the final version, this draft presents us with the same bloody puppet play.

The two anonymous bills from which I have quoted provoked a violent reaction from Bishop Larra. In a communiqué to Governor Fernández Costa, the bishop sets forth three immediate measures to be taken in pursuance of his policy of state: [1.] The arrest and imprisonment of the person or persons responsible for writing the anonymous notices; [2.] the imprisonment of Secretary Prats and the functionaries that joined him in opposing a policy which was "the only guaranty of peace";[3] and [3.] allowing the humiliation of Josefina, and not intervening militarily.

3. The issue here is the actual imprisonment of don Tomás Prats in the cells at San Felipe del Morro fortress. Prior to this order, Prats had been

Let me read to you that inflamed missive in which Larra's great Jesuitical powers seem, at last, to have waned:

Most honorable Governor of this city:
In what follows you will find, if, as I most respectfully request, you so desire, those resolutions that I deem necessary for the maintenance of the peace and tranquility of our beloved city San Juan Bautista. As the time may be close at hand when the great misfortunes that we all fear do indeed come upon us, permit me to proceed straightaway—vowing utmost clarity and distinctness in my words—to enumerate my thoughts as to the policies which I would hope to see realized in firm action immediately upon your Excellency's being apprised of them.

Item: I counsel the immediate arrest and imprisonment of those seditious citizens who, in writing and publishing abroad false statements concerning the recent events which have occupied the mind of this city, have attempted to undermine the peace and tranquility so zealously guarded and preserved by those

---

under house arrest in his own house on Caleta de la Santa Cruz, today named Caleta de las Monjas. Under Bishop Larra's order, then, possibly motivated by a deterioration in the confidence in which Bishop Larra was held by several functionaries in the colonial bureaucracy. Along with Prats, the possible conspirators don Manuel del Valle Aznar, don Sebastián Figueroa Vicente, and don Blas Foix would also be imprisoned.

humble persons upon whose heads lie the grave responsibility for leading, directing, and governing the beloved people of this city in correct and holy paths.

Item: I counsel the imprisonment of the former Secretary of State don Tomás Prats, as well as of don Manuel del Valle Aznar, don Sebastián Figueroa Vicente, and don Blas Foix. These citizens have manifested their opposition to the noble decisions which have restored peace between the two races that inhabit this our beloved island; trying the patience of the heavens, they have made statements, both publicly and secretly, in opposition to a policy which is the only guaranty of peace. Given the critical pass at which the general and ecclesiastical authorities find this island, and the terrible responsibilities of Government at such a moment, such statements are equivalent to a vile attack against the rightful and most sacred established order, and merit the makers of these statements the charge of sedition, the gravely serious nature of which charge mandating that they be immediately imprisoned until their case may be considered by the honorable Tribunal of the Indies, sitting in the capital city of New Spain.

Item: I counsel that the authorities not send any part of the island militia with orders to contain the lively popular festivities which have occupied our city upon the blessèd marriage of don Baltasar Montañez and doña Josefina Prats, and further counsel particular prudence in the care taken to ensure the safety and health of the child Josefina, and especially in all that concerns instances in which the popular cheer may, out of the esteem in which the populace holds her beloved spouse, be manifested toward her person. Take special care in transmitting unequivocal orders to the cavalry sent into the city that aggression *not* be directed against the citizenry, and be certain to have trust in the absolute loyalty and faithfulness of those troops.

Thus I transmit to my Lord Governor the above-enumerated counsels of state, and hope, in the consciousness of the benevolence of the government for my most beloved flock, for the prompt execution of these policies.

With the episcopal seal, from your humble servant,

Don José Larra,

Bishop of San Juan Bautista de Puerto Rico,

this the 15th day of June of the year of Our Lord 1753

Governor Fernández Costa's reply shows what great power Bishop Larra held within the colonial hierarchy. I think I can assert without fear of contradiction that Larra held power equivalent to that of the secretary of state or of any prime minister. Fernández Costa's letter acknowledges, and puts into effect, the three points of the policy of appeasement that Bishop Larra suggested to him. This is that singular document of compliance:

Dearest Pastor of our beloved people:

All those points counselled by your Excellency are hereby ordered to be set into action and referred to the zealous civil authorities of this city for immediate execution. It is with utmost respect that I reiterate to you the unconditional support of the military government of this city for your most happy and ingenious policy of appeasement and containment of the two principal races of our land. With this, you have my solemn vow to see that by right and force of arms, most careful and scrupulous vigilance shall be maintained with respect to all those cases in which a particular subject may act singly or in concert against the peace so zealously sought by your respected person.

All the items of counsel are hereby set in execution.

Bishop Larra always took special care to secure for himself the support of the armed forces stationed at San Felipe del Morro, that imposing fortress that guarded, and still of course guards, the bay of the city of San Juan. In this support lay all his power; but we should recall that you can do *almost* everything with a bayonet—it makes a very uncomfortable throne. In a letter from Governor Fernández Costa dated June 17, 1753, there is a clear allusion to the crisis that erupted among the military leadership due to that third suggestion, namely the prudent protection of Josefina Montañez née Prats:

Dear Pastor of our beloved flock:

In keeping with the desire for peace that animates our every official decree, we have complied with all those things counselled by your Excellency in your earlier letter to ourselves.

The civil government is even now proceeding to arrest the seditious citizens who published false, misleading, and harmful information concerning the recent festive occurrences in this city.

We are even now in pursuance of the arrest and imprisonment of don Tomás Prats and his followers in sedition. This subject has been relieved of his former detention under house arrest and has been subjected to bars and incommunication.[4]

Sra. Josefina Montañez is under our constant protection. But it is with deepest regret that I must inform you, for your ears alone, of the resistance with which that particular order has been received by our own magnificent Cavalry Corps. The young and most chaste officer Rodríguez Mora has refused to take part in the young lady's guard, unless he be given the widest latitude for action, and that of course contradicts the wise spirit of your own most prudent orders. This officer, one of the best of our beloved cavalry troops, has been taken into

---

4. This, in the official language of the eighteenth century, means that Prats was imprisoned in the dungeon (or other underground cell) of a fortress or *presidio*.

military custody until he shall have renounced his position or, should he persist in it, be brought to trial by court-martial. The young officer has been treated thus far with most benevolent prudence, and we hope that you approve our policy, given that circumstances of a most personal nature—the young man was recently promised the hand of doña Josefina Montañez—may well have altered his judgment for the worse. And because of all the foregoing events, the official arrest order has been held in abeyance. I hope that your most wise judgment may find the foregoing resolutions acceptable.

Most humbly yours,
Don Rafael Fernández Costa,
Governor of the City of
San Juan Bautista de Puerto Rico

Bishop Larra, then, encountered serious stumbling blocks to his policy. The rebellious officer mentioned by Fernández Costa was summarily executed[5] when he, along with other officers, attempted to raise a mutiny among the garrison of San Cristóbal, where he was being held. Fernández Costa's opinion that Rodríguez Mora had lost his mind when he saw his fiancée's disgrace seems correct, but there is no documentary proof of that relationship today.

---

5. The exact charges for which he was sent before the firing squad were "inciting revolt and threatening armed insurrection against authority."

When Bishop Larra was informed of the young man's death, he wrote to Governor Fernández Costa:

Youthful is the blood that is spilled in the ill-directed pursuit of selfish inclinations and not for the supreme general good. It is the nature of beardless youth, from its unique and obsessive passion, to disdain those good counsels that might avert the worst consequences of the twisted will of men. It is the nature of the barbarian to heed only his own vision, a vision nurtured by overweening pride and arrogance, and to turn a deaf ear, by this mean act, to the sublime voice which counsels that temperance and moderation which we are all obliged to impose upon the beast that lives within every human soul.

Convulsed words, these, perhaps incomprensible to, or at least not understood by, Fernández Costa, but they will help us, in my next lectures, to ferret out the mystery of Baltasar Montañez. Yes, because these words, though spoken on the occasion of Rodríguez Mora's death, spring from Larra's experience with the *enfant terrible* Baltasar.

Before bringing this first lecture to a close, I would like to read you a prose-poem by Alejandro Juliá Marín on the descent of Josefina into the mud. Its few brief words give us a keen insight into the event, bringing together all the mixed and conflicting passions we see there:

DRUNKENNESS

INNOCENCE: Baltasar! what have you done with the most delicate of flowers? You have dragged her through the mud; you have debased her purity.

BALTASAR: You are a deceitful voice. How can you exist? We are born either victims, or executioners. We are capable of enjoying the sweat, the pain, the wound of another; through fear we perpetuate men's suffering. You are a specter, or better yet, an impossible chimera, a mocking sprite. There is only the drunkenness of power or of slavery.

INNOCENCE: Heed my words: trust what all men consider proof of certainty. Doubt not that you are flesh. . . . But that is not what I care most about. I would like to ask you: Which are you? Slave, or one of the powerful?

GOD: Or are you the vilest of men, damned Baltasar! He who renounces human passions in order to achieve a world to fit his own idea. He who puts on a purity drunken with guilt, he who proclaims an innocence all too lucid. He who, renouncing my command for compassion, profits from me, and flies above me. May you be damned!

BALTASAR: Stupid, sentimental old fool! I am a man skilled in the art of fear. Some wish to save the honor of their race, some wish to humiliate, but all fear horrible scenes of death and desolation. Even the whites, therefore, wish for peace. . . . I am the hybrid bred of three chimeras, three exhausted fantasies—honor, peace, and humiliation—the three heads of slavery. They have a presentiment of blood, and possess a will for implacable control, but they are choked by fear, and they become content with the figment of power which bears my face. Who would ever have imagined that fear could accomplish so much? Once the women with children in their bellies have been kicked, and the men castrated, who will then recall the fear that once, for long eons of silence, restrained the only beast that cannot claim innocence?

Baltasar Montañez thought all this, though perhaps without such great symmetry. . . . We should recall that the nights were filled with *angelito* and the *macumbé,* and that often the flesh was clearly kindled. But revelry also breeds subtle monsters. And so Baltasar's madness begins.

LECTURE II

Good evening, my friends. Once again the mysterious figure of Baltasar Montañez will claim our attention tonight—and our detective skills, as well, to unravel the chronology of Baltasar's shadowy life is still to remain in the most limited circle of historical facts and possibilities. The descent into the enigma of Baltasar must be slow and careful; only in that way will we be able to see in his face our own, discover in his life a witness of profoundly human truths. Tonight we will look into one of the most interesting aspects of his life, which was his second renunciation. What did this renunciation consist of? Before I begin to answer that question, I should first summarize the events of his life. With those facts, I believe, we will begin to glimpse the significance of his renunciation not, this time, of his father's legacy or of his race, but his renunciation of power, and with power, the possibility of achieving peace at that convulsed moment of history.

After don Tomás Prats was imprisoned, Baltasar Montañez was made secretary of state. In chapter x of my *History and Guide to San Juan* I noted that Rafael García Gutiérrez's *Brief History of the Eighteenth Century* gives the date of Baltasar's appointment to that post as 1762—that is, after his father-in-law's death. More recent documents, and a fuller knowledge of that period, force me to reject García Gutiérrez's date. Baltasar was in fact invested with the power of the secretary of state immediately upon his father-in-law's imprisonment, and that was in the year 1753. I also asserted in my book that Baltasar began the design of his famous Garden of Afflictions sometime around 1761. Today I can rectify that date: Baltasar conceived his garden in the year 1754. This early date is documented in the following letter from Baltasar to Bishop Larra:

Most beloved Sire and Pastor—
It is with the greatest and most delight-filled hopefulness that I communicate to you, by these presents, a dream which will signify much, and bring great good, to our beloved island. This dream has planted within my soul the wondrous idea of an impregnable system of defense for our beloved city, and inspired my will with a plan for seeing this wonder realized. Herewith I inform you of that wondrous message from the heavens, that divine revelation which will make of our city the most loyal citadel and strongest bastion of our common Lord, His Majesty Charles III, King of Spain, Emperor of the Indies and the Sea—

Amidst the sweet and peaceful moments of the dawn, an angel flew to my sleeping head, and therein set the following most delicious vision: His distinguished Excellency don Baltasar Montañez, Secretary of State of the formidable City of San Juan, and Lord of the Indies, was strolling through a densely shaded

glade; about him, the little birds of the woods sang
their sweetest and most melodious songs. The thick
branches of the wood stirred in the breeze with a whisper that soothed the senses, and imparted an infinity of
pleasurable sensations to the soul of that great Lord—
who, so transported by the beauty of the place, could
but barely sustain the reins of his powerful steed. Suddenly, his marvelling eyes beheld the vision of a lovely
and well-tended garden. So he entered there, with his
companion beast, and found an imposing labyrinth of
high hedges, cul-de-sacs formed of the tall palms
known as the royal palms, and every species of vegetable prodigy. This was a vision of what we Christians
call the Earthly Paradise, before the Fall of that unfortunate wretch our father Adam. But as in that other
garden, so in this there was secreted—beneath its beautiful vestments of flowers, singing birds, the light of the
sun filtering through green leaves and fronds of lavish
exuberance—the fruit of discord and evil. Satan's
cloven hoof peeked out from the rich beauty. And it
came to pass that the most worthy don Baltasar Montañez fell into a great trap laid for him by God knows
what malevolent hand, and there found his death, for a
pit within that garden opened its vile jaws and vomited
forth thousands upon thousands of carnivorous ants,
which in short order left man and beast a skeleton. It
was then that he who was once known as Baltasar

Montañez had a most powerful revelation, which was this: That beautiful garden was a Garden of Afflictions, and none other than a most dreadful field of battle, a flowered plain which bore sure death under a guise of irresistible beauty. And this was that noble gentleman's last thought, who could already hear upon his muse's roof the scurrying of the monstrous ants, and the clicking of their magnificent jaws.

And it was this dream which brought me to lay out a Garden of Afflictions which will protect our precious realm. It shall be planted as a military defense on the tableland of El Morro Castle, and shall consist of soothing and tranquil glades and grottoes sheltering the most terrible traps: pits which flood with water, nests of poisonous or stinging creatures, and all manner of horrible fell death. This Garden shall be a part of the system of defensive walls even now being constructed, and such a combination of defenses shall be impregnable even for the most formidable of enemy. And suddenly I daresay that one day every league of our coast will enjoy the benefits of this defense, for that which this our island possesses in greatest abundance is its Nature and Nature's beauty, which we are given the opportunity to make deceitful to our ends.

This Garden shall be even more cruel than that which led our first mother and father into sin, for at that time Nature was wholly innocent, while since that dreadful time, the passage of the centuries has rendered Nature the most implacable force against which humankind is given to struggle. It is well known that plants, trees, flowers, and the sun are radiant and smiling, or dry and gloomy, without reference to the sadness or happiness of man. A day of gentle breezes and soft sun may find our soul as dark as a winter tempest. And what most fills our sight is wars, and sufferings hardly expressible in words; but those lovely countrysides, those flowered meadows which tasted blood and heard the cries of the wretched men murdered and lost in oblivion, are soon renewed, their youth returned to them by the rains and the winds, and within but a handful of years an untutored visitor who comes there will receive with incredulity the news that once there was a battle fought in that place, which destroyed an army of men and desolated even the most hidden roots of the smallest blade of grass. And thus it is that I say that Nature no longer, after the sin of our first parents, pays heed to us or our fates. Men's vanities are cruelly erased by the passing of the seasons and the eternal renewal of fauna and flora. Nature heeds not the principles, creeds, and purposes, however firm, which lead men to murder or to create, and indeed with impious cruelty makes it impossible for men to remember the glorious or ignominious deeds of ancient centuries. Thus it is, that the man who would know something of the Romans, travels not to the fields where the blood of the sons of that most powerful nation was spilled, but, if a truly wise man, goes to the ruins of the grand and magnificent monuments which still stand in the countryside about the most holy city of Rome. And I daresay that men jog their memories with the ruinous stones of ancient cities because humanity erects stones as testaments to its vanity. From this most horrifying manner of coming to that point at which deeds may be memorialized in stone— fire and blood, gunpowder exploding from cannons and harquebuses—man extracts little compassion, and indeed wrings cold comfort from marmoreal hardness, and that comfort which he does find only plays to his natural vanity. Thus, men spend all their lives in total indifference to the vegetable, mineral, and even human world—as it is perfectly natural for a man to eat with pleasure, with delight and delecta- tion, while a starving beggar puts out his empty, lep- rous hand. And so in sum—man does not seek out the history of his forebears in the green meadows or beautiful lakes which inspire such delicious sensa- tions in the present, but in ruined cities, the locus of men's vanities, the depositories and guardians of the suffering of both guilty and innocent.

And it is for all these most judicious and subtle rea- sons here expressed, that I have conceived the Garden of Afflictions as a most cruel and effective means of waging war. And I declare that henceforward I shall remain most humbly at your service in all things bearing upon this noble and most worthy plan.

We see prefigured here the visionary Baltasar who will be the object of our inquiries in my third lecture. For the moment, I only draw your attention to the overwrought, almost mystical tone through which Baltasar communicates his vision and attempts to convince the bishop of his project's feasibility. In *Illustrious Men of Our Eighteenth Century,* Marcos Rodríguez Pimentel states that at the time of Baltasar's conception of the idea of the Garden—dated by Rodríguez Pimentel, erroneously, as between 1765 and 1766—he suffered from cerebral syphilis, which was causing a progressive loss of reason. The implication is that the Garden of Afflictions is the result of this progressive insanity. Yet what is the basis of Rodríguez Pimentel's assertion? Mainly the wild and visionary tone of Baltasar's letter, supported, or so the author asserts, by an obscure medical report which mentions a syphilitic syndrome observed in Baltasar. In this report, there is no explicit mention of the "French disease," but Rodríguez Pimentel infers the disease from the symptoms displayed. I take his conclusions to be highly speculative.

There are many, many testimonies to Baltasar's degeneration, not just this letter. And when I say *degeneration,* I am not referring to the manifestation of a symptomology of syphilis, but rather to his progressive inability to exercise the power that Larra's political machinations had thrust upon him. Baltasar is no longer the man of power, but little by little has become a contemplative—his thoughts are occupied with *la condition humaine* and not with engaging the forces which lead to or sustain that condition. Baltasar's decline, if I may use that word, or "retreat," perhaps better, is accompanied by the appearance of a fascinating and mysterious figure: Juan Espinosa, an architect and leper. Baltasar's contact with this person marks the beginning of his abandonment of the world and of power, the first steps on the long road that would lead him to an understanding which, rising above power and the wellspring of power, compassion, resulted from a harsh and severe fidelity.

The progress of this radical change in him is chronicled, as I say, in a wealth of anecdotes and a veritable storehouse of documents. There is time to look at only a small part of them, those that the years have proven to be the most useful in understanding the character and work of Baltasar.

One of these sources, little known and even less commented on, is a collection of drawings by Juan Espinosa. Let us pause, before we embark on that journey which will take us to the dark castle of that second Baltasar Montañez, to look for a moment at those drawings. They lie today in the Municipal Archives of the city of San Juan. No doubt the reason for their scholarly neglect, the reason they have not been studied, or even very often mentioned, is their scabrous and shocking subject matter, for they contain graphic scenes of the orgies which Baltasar celebrated in the private apartments of the the Palace of State. These drawings are of utmost importance in plumbing the psychological and spiritual depths of that Baltasar who married "the loveliest flower of Island society" on that fateful June 1, 1753.

From the beginning, the marriage was marked by the impossibility of achieving what we would call today "a healthy relationship": She had been forced into the marriage by reasons of state; he had agreed to it in order to be free of the dead hand of his father that lay so heavy upon him. The black man was raised up, honored with the hand of a white woman of high estate; in turn, he was to be grateful. But Baltasar was far too intelligent to play that role. He grasped its ultimate significance perfectly, and took immediate refuge in an attitude of belligerence and aggression. The well-calculated "dragging through the mud" of Josefina demonstrated his will to humiliate the white race, to satisfy to some degree the yearning for revenge felt by not a few black men whose women had been raped and violated by the capricious lust of the slave master. He attempted to sully the white child's wedding gown, plant his seed in that belly where Hispanic honor begins and ends.

Baltasar's pride, however, prevented him from consummating the act with Josefina. He recognized that he was a victimizer held in contempt by his victim; his pleasure would in Josefina's eyes be his humiliation. He renounced the body of his beautiful wife, for a carnal relationship with her would have brought the powerful humiliation through the scorn and contempt of the weak. And the possibility of humiliation existed because of a terrible secret that lurked deep in his psyche: his fear of a latent tendency to acknowledge his inferiority to the white master. Josefina's body became, in his own words, a "temptation to inferiority." Throughout the diary he kept, we find testimony to Baltasar's subtle and equivocal sexual attitude toward Josefina. This is the entry for September 4, 1753:

I told my confessor, the most venerable Bishop don José Larra, that I have not yet consummated marriage with my honored wife doña Josefina Prats, to which my confessor replied with a most subtle smile: "With this renunciation you have achieved that which don Tomás Prats feared he would betray with his."[1] We both laughed, applauding that happy sally of wit; but that night I did not sleep, having awakened to the irony that

1. That is: With your renunciation of carnal union with Josefina you have preserved the young woman's purity—the purity that Tomás Prats, her father, attempted to preserve when he refused to renounce his firm resove not to allow the marriage.

I had joined the most subtle bishop in mocking my own condition. I was assailed by a whirlwind of apprehensions. Did that mitered serpent mean that I, after all that has occurred, served the desires of a man who despised me for my race, or in other words, that I preserved his daughter's virginity, honoring like the faithful slave his master's wishes?

Baltasar's cynical turn of mind led him to terrible questions, and the origin of these questions was his deep-rooted yet largely unacknowledged sense of inferiority. In another passage we read: "I have never set eyes on those parts which modesty has banished to invention.[2] Within me the desire of an entire race cries out, yet it is not a desire for pleasure, but rather a desire to humiliate. And it is for that reason that I fear that when I mount her I shall meet a glacial look of hatred which will make me see the weakness of my attempt." Baltasar recognized the inability of the black man—inheritor of the slave's passions and the slave's psychology—to truly humiliate the white. Baltasar had to be supremely clever, and take great care, for what he wished to do was humiliate Josefina without wounding the Satanic pride which inspired him.

And indeed he achieved this end on February 22, 1754, as we read in his diary:

2. "Imagination."

And I shall install in her bedchamber a tiny spyglass in a peephole opening onto my pleasure retreat,[3] and this peephole will be a permanent temptation during those fantasy-filled nights when through the trumpets[4] her ears hear sounds which will lead her mind to invent the most rubicund and delicious pleasures of the flesh. She will hear the sounds, the soft noise of panting which writhing bodies emit from the immense pleasure which is that of the flesh, and then she will want to join our orgies; but that will be possible only by the sense of sight, and this shall be her sweet humiliation, that bends her body to my iron will without my suffering the torment of her gaze. Our conjugal love shall be achieved in the solitary pleasure to which she is inspired by the celestial music of my well-accompanied frenzy.

In these words we hear the tone almost of madness that will progressively characterize Baltasar's utterances—perhaps his very soul. But we must not reduce this "alienation," as an earlier generation might have called it, to such physiological causes as syphilis; I see it as the product of Baltasar's ongoing struggle with his genius and his vision.

3. This was how Baltasar referred to the room in which he celebrated his frenzied orgies.

4. Small megaphones, like hearing trumpets, which would carry the erotic sounds from Baltasar's chamber into Josefina's.

Let us begin our descent into "mad Baltasar" with those drawings by Juan Espinosa. These erotic, if you will, drawings translate the frenzy and wildness of that tortured soul.

The first drawing takes us inside Baltasar's chamber, shows us the rococo style in which the "retreat of delights" is decorated. Lying on his enormous bed, Baltasar, his private parts naked, caresses the genitals of five beautiful ladies of pleasure. On each side of Baltasar, Espinosa has painted two generously proportioned female backsides, four in all, all naked. Baltasar manipulates the mounts of Venus of these women, and with his tongue, stimulates that of a fifth who stands at the head of the bed. The position of the female backsides in the upper background of the drawing produces a rhythmic balance in the composition, and the sensuality of the scene is emphasized by its isolation and its great difference in tone from the other images portrayed. In the foreground of the drawing, Juan Espinosa sits at an easel painting the orgy. In the chamber next door, Josefina is embroidering beside the window; her gaze falls on the beautiful tropical landscape outside. On the other side of Baltasar's chamber lies Bishop Larra's study, and beside his desk stands the page Rafael González Pimentel. As some of us may recall from our history classes, the young González Pimentel was orphaned when his parents died in the wreck of the *Ponsa* in 1738, and later in his life he became the influential secretary to Bishop Trespalacios. In this panel of the drawing, Bishop Larra is writing in his diary, and behind him we see Sor Inés de los Benditos, Bishop Larra's housekeeper. For each of these portraits Alejandro Juliá Marín has written a "meditation"; these are his commentaries on the first drawing:

THE PROFLIGATES

Far in the background in the central chamber, Baltasar surrenders to a pleasure which hides, behind a veil of obscene whispers, the face of the defenseless unfortunate who wanders on his crutches through the world's rain and cold.

Josefina distracts herself with only the nervous cooing of the doves fluttering in the sun.

The Bishop draws plans for the dwelling place men ask of God, but those closest to him, like that boy-child with dark ringlets and blue eyes, whisper darkly to us of other things: night after night, it seems, they rush to the pain of unrequitedness, the misery of failure....

In the second drawing Juan Espinosa does not appear, but his cape, wide-brimmed hat, and drawing instruments are lying on a chair in the foreground. In Baltasar's chamber there is sheer, unbridled orgy: in the center of his huge bed, our hero performs cunnilingus on a lady who is doing the same to another, and this second to a third, and so on, forming a half-moon of pleasure—until the last in the chain performs violent fellatio on the dark male. In the next room

Josefina is sitting, very close to the wall which separates her apartment from Baltasar's, embroidering. In Bishop Larra's study, Sor Inés is reading her breviary next to the wall which protects her from the sight of the erotic abandon taking place only inches from her, while Bishop Larra is calibrating a series of small spyglasses (the same used for inserting into peepholes drilled between rooms), and the page has his ear to the wall. This is Juliá Marín's meditation on this drawing:

REPORT ON EROTIC CUSTOMS . . .

The ancients exalted hearing above all other senses, and explained that in death, it was this sense which was the last to leave the dying man, the last relic of life. . . .

Many refined persons in those distant times believed that being heard in the raptures of their ecstasy lent the most exquisite sauce to their delights. The calloused hands of servants brought low by the dream of lustful genitals. . . .

And moreover, in that way power would prevail to the verge of its own ruin.

The third drawing has Baltasar in the full act of intercourse with a mulatto woman who will appear again in the next two scenes. (This is Juana, Juan Espinosa's daughter. Upon the painter's death, Baltasar took her into his house as a maid.) While Baltasar makes love to her, Juana performs cunnilingus on a white woman wearing a hood. We can easily guess the identity of this voluptuary: she is, I believe, Josefina Montañez née Prats, and I will try to prove my hypothesis in this way. In the previous scenes, the painter has suggested that Josefina becomes gradually more interested in the erotic sounds that come from her husband's chamber next door. In this one, Josefina is sitting in her room on a small divan, masturbating as she spies on Baltasar's orgy through a peephole. (This peephole, of course, is the same one mentioned by Baltasar in his diary, and probably was fitted with a spyglass belonging to the well-focused collection that Bishop Larra maintained for spying on his collaborators and assistants.)[5] The process is clear: The lascivious and tempting sounds of the orgies have seduced Josefina's imagination, and it is this seduction, or the power of the young woman's imagination, that Espinosa is suggesting in his drawing. The white woman in the hood, that is, who is pleasured by Juana's cunnilingus, is Josefina's excited fantasy. The "good little girl" has been transported by her own imagination to Baltasar's bed, and has turned what was simple coitus into unbridled orgy. But Espinosa's drawing has other subtle touches: In the foreground, spying

5. A typical custom of the Spanish baroque. These spyglasses, known as "ubiquities," inserted into peepholes, were introduced by Philip II, king of Spain (r. 1598–1621), in his years of intrigue against Antonio Pérez. They are sometimes, therefore, known in Spanish as *"antonietas."* Their usefulness was still recognized during the reign of Alfonso XII (r. 1874–1885).

from behind a curtain, we find the young page González Pimentel. As he is caressing his erect member in an act of masturbation, he presents us his naked backside. Then there is Bishop Larra's study: In the background, Sor Inés is lying on a couch, her face showing clear signs of ecstasy. Her private parts are hidden behind a screen, but the reason for her rapture seems clear enough—near her, we see an *"antonieta"* like that in Josefina's chamber. Meanwhile, Bishop Larra is sitting in his confessional. He is apparently sitting for his portrait, since his right hand holds a scroll with the motto *Ego sum pastor bonus.* His thick crosier, or shepherd's crook, terminates in a curled penis. This is Juliá Marín's poetic commentary on this third drawing:

FALSIFICATION

And finding himself in a countryside of a thousand eyes, Andrenius asked, "What is this wonder which my eyes behold?"

To which the sage Crityllus replied: "They are the eyes of power, which spy upon man from the moment of his birth, when his mother's entrails still twine about his body, and follow him through all this great countryside of slavery which the ancients called the labyrinth of good order."

But Andrenius did not grasp the customs. . . . "Dear teacher," he said, "can you not reveal to me the mysteries of this astounding vision?"

And that enlightened man gave his reply:

"Some avenues in this labyrinth," he said, "are extremely narrow from the shoulders to the eyes; you will find in these strait passages men with small heads, unfortunate wretches whose reason is guided by the map and compass of the powerful. But you will also find, in these same passages, men with enormously swollen heads. Be most vigilant for these figures, who are like great malign diseases that in deepest night possess the body. And that watch you keep will show you how, while the first men live under the oppression of their opposites, these latter live in subjection to a slavery cast over themselves by themselves and their futile reasoning. The first live in taciturnity, the second in a tendency toward logorrhea. And from these observations, we may infer: Cultivate small reasoning, and you shall never fail of occasions. The second avenue or passage through this labyrinth is that called the *pectoralis*; and this name is given it for the fact that in it those who suffer persecution from their own bodies slither and drag themselves along it, look up at the slave, and declare How broad is his chest, how brave his respiration! The third avenue is that of the man who lives under an obsession with the gifts of the table—look how his chest is fallen, and how quickly his soul flies from him! And now you will find the magnificent avenue of those who spend their breath in the most occult and hidden delights. These feel a heavy force which drags them downward, downward, until they fall into the supreme delight, my beloved, my soft and delicate Andrenius. . . ."

THE COLLECTOR

Rapt by delicious ecstasy, he looks out at us from his pretended wait. Inside, all dreams lie like tiny curled-up animals, and his desires journey through regions of compassion (thoughts which acknowledge the supreme necessity of other men). But it happens that with such abandon one unrolls, untwists, and the flesh comes alive behind the power, awaiting the witness of another person's delights, storing away in coffers and diminutive golden caskets those moans and cries which are the most precious trophies of his infinite collection of passions, worthy of a cathedral.

In the penultimate drawing, Baltasar is lying on his enormous bed, smoking a long pipe. At the foot of the bed is Juana. Above Baltasar's head Juan Espinosa has painted a little cloud which contains a part of the landscape of the Garden of Afflictions. This touch suggests that the conception of the Garden derives from the use of a narcotic.[6] In the next room, Josefina lets her eyes roam

6. We can easily presume, though we have no documentary proof, that Baltasar was addicted to the mildly hallucinogenic plant called *perico,* a

over a nocturnal landscape. The window has become very narrow. In Bishop Larra's office, we see the following scene: Larra is sitting in the confessional. He is hearing a young lady's confession, and his hand is beneath his habit. We may assume that the young woman is Josefina, though we are not at all certain of that, since she is hidden by the curtain of the confessional.[7] Waiting to confess are the boy González Pimentel and Sor Inés, Josefina's companions in the solitary vice which so fills the previous drawing. We believe—and the mannerist style, typical of Juan Espinosa, supports our belief—that Espinosa wished to suggest Josefina's madness by means of her double appearance in this drawing. Let us hear the varied and profound musings of Alejandro Juliá Marín on this design:

HEARD LANDSCAPE

"Is that some wretched thud on the paving stones of the plaza? Was that a long drawn-out scream? The dim light barely penetrates my navel. My temples yield under the narrow file of cares which sweep me to the sole idea. For me, all is now closed. Behind me lie our lust, my slavery,

---

plant which has been utterly eradicated from our flora. Juan Espinosa used this drug in order to bear the pain of his disease.

7. We take the female to be young because of her shoes, which are of a type called *"alzados,"* or "elevated," much the fashion among young peninsular Spanish ladies of the early eighteenth century.

and we love without the consent of our wills. Two doves free in the light.... Never more will their gazes meet; the intimate touch which in Baltasar remains distracted is born to death. Enwrapped in tenderness, our intentions will not cross in this well-mapped labyrinth."

THE GAZE

Men are so bewitched by the flesh that they hardly can foresee the theft. But sometimes it happens that in the night, someone does hold back, and watches over the entire estate.

Those who have awakened to darkness have seen a long murmur of eyes alighting on the world. The most exaggerated of them have even claimed that they hear someone hammering in the highest spheres, and they repeat as though in a dream, "Yes, it was as though someone were hammering nails, up on the roof of a house."

Several nights passed without the watch, but in time the light brush of those universal eyes returned. And then there were many who awoke with a start from their sleep; they were awakened by that booming.... After all, the time lost had to be recovered.

From the sky, dolls fell, with pleasuring holes. This entertained the men, but it hardly made an impression on the children, who insisted, these enemies of the people, upon forming committees which stood watch over the gigantic spotlights which lit the construction site. Ingenuity had not a moment of creative solitude; the dolls soon grew tiresome; tedious curiosity awoke once more.

FANTASIES LIE WEARIED

All things grow tiresome, and even the shepherd at times feels a certain curiosity about the ewes.

He required them to tell their most private and delicious details—("Not a spot of sin must remain in your soul. Forgiveness must extend to every darkest corner. Satan's cleverness knows no bounds, and he lays his snares in forgotten places. Make an effort, my daughter!").

And thus it was—in the inviolable secrecy of the confessional—that he amassed his collection. The catalog was abandoned; there existed curiosities relegated to the oblivion of men. In a word, all lay wearied, and the inquisitions hardly served for a dangerously domestic lust. (Her own lechery sated from so many rites, Sor Inés cauterized her entrails with a lighted candle.)

That cathedral of delicacies, tidbits, and exquisite morsels exhausted human caprice.

DECADENCE

For a long time he held back from the excesses that enslave men. But the exquisite gifts of recent years have made him forget time, which is life pushing onward, and little by little his power has dribbled away.

The last of the drawings portrays the following scene: Baltasar has left his bed and is making his way toward a large window, which has not appeared in any of the previous drawings. From there, he can contemplate the magnificent Garden of Afflictions and its beauties. Juana is clutching at his legs, though Baltasar is indifferent to his lover's pleas. The pipe is abandoned on the bed. Our hero stands absorbed in contemplation of the countryside; his eyes, his ears are hardly part of this world. Josefina's chamber is utterly deserted. And a curious detail—the window has disappeared. All this prophesies the future desolation of the house of Baltasar Montañez. To the other side, in Bishop Larra's study, we come upon a true enigma: We see, for the first time, an obstetrical chair—a birthing bed. Sor Inés, the nun, is lying on it. The bishop is embracing her in furious sexual frenzy. Behind Bishop Larra, sodomizing him, is the page González Pimentel. The expressions on all three faces are that of frank erotic ecstasy. It is odd, but in this scene the figures are all fully clothed. Why did Espinosa portray them this way? Might it be out of respect for ecclesiastical dignity?

The last interesting detail of this scene is the double appearance of the bishop. He appears in the orgiastic scene I have just described, and also appears knocking on Baltasar's door.

This is what Juliá Marín wrote about this last drawing:

ALL IS CLOSED

The first thing was the window. It gradually shrank, and toward the end it could hardly hold the landscape of screaming that trickled like a tear. The story of her life is barely known, but it would not be hard to guess: radiant light flooding the cooing of the doves in flight, and then the shadow of a strange bird never seen in those skies. Heavy eyelids that gravitate in silence toward the round navel.

THE MEETING

All of Greece was talking about a young man beautiful and wise named Diogenes.

Hallucinating from the sweet herbs brought from the Ganges, a general led his armies along difficult routes, long detours that put off the day of their arrival home. Silence would descend over the camp; only the night would observe those tired eyes that dreamed of the meeting: "Diogenes is a man of utmost beauty, and there is talk that on one particular day his gravity is laid aside for the most delicious games. His thoughts are scattered in caresses, blue-eyed ephebes surrender to the sad gaze of the man prematurely wise. But night is running fast; only Diogenes remains awake, and he counts the overturned cups, the naked bodies, the ringlets that dream of rough beards. Toward dawn, his sandals are heard; the fool returns to his corner."

Two days the army spent in surrounding the humble hut. The great man asked what the sweet day was. . . .

On the eve of that day, he adorned his temples with laurel, set perfumed jasmine about his loins, a garland of daisies about his waist, and covered his nakedness with a wide purple cape.

Just before sunrise, a nervous guard accompanied him to the wise man's hut. But the place was empty. A stammering shepherd pointed toward the mountain top.

What sweet moments, anticipated lovemaking!

Five hundred of the most loyal and courageous men surrounded the entrance to the cave. The great man pulled back the cloth that covered the door, but the hard face of the sun barely touched those distracted eyes. The dimness returned, weary in the circle of a torch.

Alexander let fall his cape.

The voice of Diogenes was heard: "Get out of the way, you're blocking the sun."

The most powerful man on earth picked up his mantle. The night lasted many days; the long weeping adulterated the wine in his cup; the lord of the earth moaned as he gnawed heavy skins. But no one knew. (Power's concessions to emotions can be fatal.)

The young lord died, and it was then that the mystery of that meeting was understood:

"What a racket armies make!"

Construction on the Garden of Afflictions began in 1766. Juan Espinosa was the garden's first victim. He died in the construction of an immense crab which would protect the northeast flank of the Garden. (According to some witnesses, the leprous architect committed suicide by closing up all the exits from the monster built of plaster of Paris and the shells of crustaceans.) But soon that vision of a cursed and twisted Nature would begin to claim a long list of victims. Baltasar Montañez, the visionary himself, the creator of the "vegetable traps," our hero, was the first of these unfortunates.

In August 1767 the Inquisition declared the Garden of Afflictions "a prodigy of Satan." This declaration was a shot aimed at Baltasar Montañez' political career. It was not the Inquisition's intention merely to destroy the visionary's military project; also, and indeed principally, the intention was to destroy Baltasar's and Bishop Larra's political power. Those who sympathized with former Secretary of State Prats saw their constant intrigues against his interlopers crowned with success. In the Admonishment[8] published by the Holy Tribunal on September 3, 1767, the "criminal actions" taken by Baltasar Montañez are summarized in this way:

We find the accusation of the citizenry against the honor-

8. The edict of condemnation published by the Inquisition's Holy Tribunal was titled thus.

able Secretary of State don Baltasar Montañez to be true, and in view of the truth of that accusation, and by virtue of the divine assistance granted us by the Estates of the Indies, we pronounce the following judgment most fell:

It is the resolution of this council and the solemn judgment of the most Holy Church of the Indies, in extension of the Holy Roman and Catholic Church, that the following acts, which offend against the evident truths of the One True Religion, be revealed, in the fervent wish that by so doing this council may merit the blessing of our Father ever watchful and jealous of the truths spoken by His Son made flesh through the Most Holy Virgin Mary, ourselves having called upon the name of Christ, and having before our eyes God only, the purity of the orthodox faith, and the unity of the Holy Catholic Church.

It is for advocating doctrine beyond the pale of the Holy Catholic Church and every true and correct interpretation of the Gospels, for having permitted his conscience to stray outside the teachings of received and revealed Tradition, and beyond all acts of Revelation, that we declare the person of Baltasar Montañez, who occupies in this the king's city of San Juan Bautista of the island of Puerto Rico the position of Secretary of State, to be a heterodox subject of King Charles III of Spain, to be a pestilential assertor of perverse doctrines, and to be a rebel and opposed to the authority and power of the Catholic Church. We declare that he is, moreover, a manifest heretic and that, an obstinate and manifest heretic. We pronounce the causes of said subject's heterodoxy to be the following actions and volitions: said Baltasar Montañez has instituted false worship of certain Gardens destined to that destruction belonging properly to warfare, for which reason vileness and perversion may be inferred in the conception which said subject holds with regard to the high order and beauty of the Divine Plan, and he is willful and unrepentant of this falseness. The subject Baltasar Montañez is therefore condemned for sin *horrendis naturae*, and shall hereby be damned for all eternity in person, work, and shared intellectual descendants. We do relax[9] him to the arm and judgment of the secular court, affectionately requesting the said court, that they should so moderate their sentence as not to involve death or the mutilation of his members.

Done in offering to the Glory of God.

Baltasar's excommunication is cloaked in the mantle of

9. This apparently modern word was the technical term used when the authorities of the Church, who could only intervene in spiritual matters, cast the heretic from the fold and "turned him over" to the civil authorities for civil "processing." Since the guilty party was no longer a member of society as constituted by the laws of God, he had of necessity to be banished or otherwise disposed of, as by burning. This "relaxation," therefore, was a most serious, and terrible, measure.

theology in order to disguise its true cause. And naturally the Inquisition came up against some hard resistance from Bishop Larra, who refused to stand idly by as his brilliant plan was destroyed by his protégé's dementia and his enemies' slow but effective intrigues. He did everything in his power to prevent the civil authorities from issuing the order for Baltasar's immediate arrest that the Inquisition demanded. I will read to you from a second document, in which the Holy Tribunal makes its will known with respect to Baltasar's imprisonment:

> For the execution of that which pertains appropriately to the civil authorities of these Kingdoms, we defer to the secular arm of governance in the issuance of the edict of suspension of said subject's civil guarantees, which action we require *instanter*. We furthermore require [*i.e.*, demand] the privation of said subject's movement by means of immediate imprisonment, allowing the subject within said privation sufficient air to breathe in order to maintain his life. By these presents we require and so CERTIFY with this PONTIFICAL SEAL, executed in these KINGDOMS OF THE INDIES, the denial to said subject of all horizontal volition, leaving however to him vertical volition so that thereby, by divine and beneficent grace, he may be brought to the truth which lies Above.

Bishop Larra replied to this order with a brief and most ingenious letter in which he explains to the island's governor his reasons for opposing Baltasar's imprisonment. This is the bishop's note:

Respected sir:

Word having come to my ear that the most Holy Tribunal of this island has decreed a sentence of excommunication and damnation against the king's subject and present Secretary of State don Baltasar Montañez, and furthermore that the Holy Tribunal has required that this worthy person be immediately imprisoned, I find myself in a most humble state, in which I must both lament and give warning. I lament because I believe that the Holy Tribunal has exceeded those prerogatives of vigilance which the Code of the Indies confers, by custom and usage, to the General Dispositions of the Ecclesiastical Realm. And I give warning because of my most certain conviction that the imprisonment of the subject Baltasar Montañez will lead inevitably to desolation and war upon the recently pacified lands of our beloved island. Our memory must not fail, at this delicate moment of state, to recall that the marriage of Baltasar Montañez to Josefina Prats has restored our most beloved flock to a state of spiritual and material peace, and a great sweetness and concord between the races. The body of state will, I believe, inevitably be scourged by the disease of violence and sedition if the condition of executive privilege, accorded by custom, right, and due to the most worthy person of the present Secretary of State, be altered by action or intention. It is for these reasons that I state my desire and issue stern order that the Holy Tribunal desist from its demand for imprisonment and the execution of that demand, and do so for most grave reasons of state; noting, nevertheless, my acknowledgment of, and abstention from participation in all things respecting, the theological process which pertains solely and uniquely to that Tribunal, as the Instrument and Arm of the Holy See in the Kingdoms of the Indies.

But this time Bishop Larra's "grave reasons of state" did not receive the same support as on other occasions. The Holy Tribunal resorted to blackmail, in fact, in order to dissuade the prelate from his objections to Baltasar's imprisonment. What sort of blackmail? The Inquisition threatened to send Rome word of Josefina Prats's forced marriage to Baltasar, and of Bishop Larra's role as principal architect of that union. It also threatened to communicate to Rome and the colonial authorities its protest against the removal and imprisonment of the former secretary of state, don Tomás Prats. Let me read you a bit of the blackmail note:

Having received your correspondence of this day concerning the finding of guilt and execution of judgment against this Crown's and this Church's subject don Baltasar Montañez, we lift from the following events, which offend against episcopal and theological integrity, the silence which has enveloped them since their recent commission; further, we advise Your Worship that information of these events will be sent to the Holy See should you continue in your present indisposition toward the supreme theological authority of this Tribunal. The events which still rankle in our memory surely will be fresh still in your own, and so we but briefly DECLARE:

That it was against the will of the maiden Josefina Prats that matrimony both ecclesiastical and civil was contracted with her for purported reasons of state, abominable and contemptible reasons to which political men and self-proclaimed statesmen, who use the word of God to justify human passions, have eternally appealed. And also:

That the author of this offense against the integrity of the sacrament of matrimony was in fact and in deed your Eminence, Bishop don José Larra, so titled by the most Holy See of the Church-Delegate of the New Indies.

We inform you also of the most courageous opposition directed by the father of Josefina Prats through the channels by which such protests are brought to the diocese and the Holy Inquisition; opposition which, however, by reason of the general air of Machiavellian intrigue in which canonical law and right are most egregiously violated, received only the most decided and cruel repulse, in the form of the expulsion from office of said don Tomás Prats, Secretary of State of this realm of the Catholic King Charles III of Spain, with the addition of that subject's arbitrary and unforewarned imprisonment.

It is for all the above-mentioned reasons, that should Bishop don José Larra persist in his erroneous opinions regarding the theological finding of guilt, the excommunication, and the damnation of the subject Baltasar Montañez, this Holy Tribunal shall proceed with the presentation of ecclesiastical facts before the Supreme See of the Holy Church in Rome, and with the protest and information of facts before the Most Wise and Venerable Royal Council of the Indies and before the Emperor of the Indies himself, his Majesty Charles III, King of Spain, jewel of the authority which for hundreds of years God has maintained in these Indies in the service of the Holy Catholic and most orthodox Church, its daughter in faith and in defense, the land of Spain.

SO DECREED, UNDER THE SIGN OF THE CROSS, FOR THE DECEASED.[10]

10. This phrase means that what is spoken, written, or ordered here is decreed for all people, even for the dead. This figure of speech, here of course translated, was brought into Spanish protocol-language through Austrian influence, and it may be seen in the "boilerplate" of the Austrian Empire down to the time of Bismarck.

It goes without saying that Baltasar Montañez was arrested and imprisoned forthwith. Bishop Larra did, however, manage to see that his protégé was not removed from the high office he occupied. He was allowed to keep his title as a guarantee of racial peace. In case of some future Negro revolt, the prelate won the concession that Baltasar would be restored to his position.

In January 1768, Baltasar Montañez was "interned" in the fortress of San Felipe del Morro. The government's official historian relates the events which surrounded his imprisonment:

Amidst mutinies and cries of fury from mobs of angry Negroes within this capital of insular government and throughout the countryside around it, the heretic subject Baltasar Montañez was interned today in the Crown's fortress San Felipe del Morro. A troop of mounted cavalry and lancers accompanied the episcopal carriage which transported the Secretary of State to his place of present and permanent residence. The entire route of march along the rocky coastline known as Miramar had to be cleared, by repeated charges of the royal infantry and the insular cavalry, of the thousands of Negroes who with suicidal wilfulness attempted to free the man they have denominated the "child Malumbi."[11]

11. In the cult of *santería* widespread in Cuba and Puerto Rico, Malumbi is a mischievous minor deity who, rebelling against Changó, freed the captive Eneayá, the goddess of fantasy, dancing, and forgetfulness.

The rocks along the coast still evidence their dead and abandoned bodies. The caravan of mounted and infantry troops maintained a slow but firm march, clearing the roadway of the successive mobs which like savage waves of surf broke across it. The most blessèd authority of the Indies went before, and behind there were left lying in hillocks along the route the inert bodies of savages who, recognizing neither true authority nor its instruments, attempted most impiously to violate the will of Christ as made known through His vicars and defenders here on Earth, the Holy Inquisition and its most worthy councilors. On occasion, the caravan was obliged to halt, or could only move forward with great difficulty. In the end, three days were required to travel the short distance between the Palace of State, the place of Baltasar Montañez' detention, and the most magnificent fortress San Felipe del Morro. Often there spread the rumor that the carriage which bore the condemned man had stopped, and was unprotected, as the cavalry and infantry protecting it had been dispersed; but it is our certain knowledge that such rumors, as that the accursèd prisoner attempted to escape, are wholly without truth or foundation, and that of the few savages who reached the carriage, the wounds of their dead bodies are at this moment washed by the waters of the ocean that crashes on the rocks of the coast of Miramar, or have become nauseating food for the many fearsome sharks who swim along that littoral.

Our wandering friend Alejandro Juliá Marín pauses before that scene of carnage:

THE PROCESSION

He is drawn on, and there is heard in his wake the sound of gaping bellies uttering cries of blood and entrails. Above these huge mouths of pain, endless spears, whose work of killing is never finally done, still flash in the sun. All lies shattered, broken, ruined, dead. . . .

He is alone now. Distracted from his single-minded obsession, he meditates on a noisy cavalry charge, troops pursuing the blacks toward the distant precipices. He puzzles over the music of harquebuses, and he wonders what that penetrating odor is. There is hardly a sound. This is the moment to escape.

But his wearied gaze has returned again to silence, and his masterful fingers draw, with delicate touch, a misguided Garden in the dense air. The sky's face is inscrutable.

The imprisonment of the popular hero Baltasar Montañez set off an unprecedented wave of indignation in the black population. Bands of guerrillas roamed the mountains. The great sugarcane plantations of Monte Hatillo, Ensenada Vieja, Laguna de Cocos, and Sabana Nueva were attacked. Almost the entire sugar cane harvest that year was burned by the hordes of enraged blacks. The wealthy hacienda owners and their families fled before the heart-stopping cry of *¡Viva Baltasar!* and the inferno that succeeded it. Those blacks loyal to their masters, the so-called "coconuts" who were black on the outside, white on the inside, were brutally murdered by the bands of revolutionaries. One chronicler of the time, the private assistant to the Ministry of State and Civil Affairs, paints this horrible and macabre scene:

> I describe the sight out of sacred duty, for did duty not demand it, my pen would freeze at the supreme terror which my eyes have witnessed, a terror only conceivable in the will of these Negroes whose nature the divine plan makes as wild beasts, and who, unable to comprehend how education may make them human, abandon themselves to their fiercest, yet most natural, instincts.
>
> For many leagues before arriving at the estate of don Alvaro San Sebastián, we were obliged to suffer a most nauseating stench, wafted throughout those desolate acres by the soft breezes of July. Everything about us had been burned. League upon league of rich sugar cane had been rendered ashes by the infinite bestiality of this race. Even the coconut palms, with their hard and resistant wood, had been swept away by the implacable waves of that sea of flame. The sky was black with sulfurous smoke. That air, which one could with but difficulty breathe, dense as it was with smoke and filled with

clouds of ashes, was resistant also to the sense of sight. Few were the outlines discernible in that inferno worthy of a Dante or a Hieronymus Bosch. But hardly was there need of sight for one to grasp the horrible scene that spread before us. The stench, as I say, was unbearable; we had come to a place which had seen most dreadful pain, most horribly unbridled acts of slaughter. Hundreds of rotting and dismembered bodies lay piled upon the fields, a plain—nay, a mountain—of suffering, a burial mound of the unburied! May God give me strength to tell what mine eyes have seen, so that men may nevermore yield to the temptation to alter what the divine hand has disposed. Oh God! All the heads were piled on the top of the mound, but they were heads without eyes, without noses, without ears. Then, descending toward the base of this horrific pyramid of the dead, a tangled mass of grotesquely mutilated bodies: feet disjoined from their legs, limbs torn from trunks, and all, garnished with jewels of the most willed and intended cruelty, an embroidery of contempt which even the vilest of Christians would never have been capable of—for that pile of rotting flesh, blood, and broken and twisted bones was circled by garlands made of female breasts and masculine members. And yet that hellish "adornment," worthy of a demon more terrible than Satan, paled beside the bloody female pubes rammed into the likewise bloody mouths of the unfortunate victims. Oh, how can one ever hope to expunge from memory the vision of that monument to misery and infinite human wickedness! Happy, I thought, the victims whose eyes were pulled out before they could look upon this tree on which the basest expression of fallen human nature, the heretical race of idolatrous savages, has set, with the care and artistry of their perverse reason, the most subtle trophies of their unspeakable malignity, their fierce yet degenerate condition!

Yet that thought was but a child's prefiguration of the bitter reflections to which I was obliged—what a terrible responsibility was mine!—by an even more horrible scene not far from the place I have just described.

I must beg forgiveness if the knot which comes again to my throat with the terrible remembrance of that horrific and ignominious sight should manifest itself in my pen, and make it even more difficult and laborious for the men and women who may read this, to conceive the infinite evil of these beings who ever afterward shall have so little claim to the appellative "human," notwithstanding that the divine will has bestowed upon the creatures the semblance of humanity, albeit in a shade of blackness which can only confirm the general suspicion of their hellish tendencies, and of their possessing a terrible void where in us the soul resides.

Oh my God, give me strength to carry out my humble task, which is to chronicle these horrors—

Not far, as I have indicated, from that noisome mountain of limbs and entrails—for one cannot call them men and women—we came to the ancestral home of the wealthy plantation owner don Rafael Montoya Cambó. As the stench grew ever more unbearable as we approached the half-destroyed house, we were forced, so as not to faint, to tie handkerchiefs over our noses and mouths. The first obstacle we encountered when we attempted to set foot on the grand portico of the mansion, was a chain of human intestines strung, like those velvet ropes used by officers who enforce order in official celebrations, across the entire front, from column to column of the stately porch, and hung also from the roof beams. At last we made access into the house itself, which had once been a thing of such beauty, and into the parlor which once had witnessed the lovely steps of the dancing ladies, the delicate roses of their cheeks, and the genteel importunings of the gentlemen for their hands in a dance. What vile contrast was there! Oh credulous times, that can trust the venomous black serpent that feeds in the barracks, and fail to remember the awful wickedness and evil of which mankind is capable! Now is when my pen indeed sticks—for what horror! On top of the daughter Carmencita's piano we discovered the decapitated head of noble don Rafael, and in its mouth, stuffed there most savagely, his private organs. Lying upon the mansion's great divan we found don Rafael's naked torso, which had been placed in a most obscene posture, with its backside in the air, and tied to it—oh God!—the head of his faithful Negro overseer. So extreme had been the unspeakable barbarity committed here that almost the entire tongue of the unfortunate servant—a good black man, one of those who accept with blessed patience and docility their condition, and give thanks to God for the great favor which He has bestowed upon them, of living among a race which rears them up to Christianity and humanity; a man who, though black like the vile seditious crew which had performed these deeds of unutterable inhumanity, found that his color availed him naught with them—into that part of his master's body which decorum begs me not name. Near this most horrid and regrettable scene, we found the mutilated body of her who, in her days of dolls and dances,[12] had been the most famous beauty of the colony, the sweet child Carmencita. This child bore bruises across her entire body, and the marks of pummeling and pinching; and this was a clear sign of the violation to which she had been subjected before being borne to the farthest poles of outrage. The ultimate violation was that of a torch introduced still flaming into her venereal parts. Her head, set among the crystal teardrops of what had been the most magnificent chandelier of this

12. The balls of society, that is.

island, was not found until night was well advanced. And that lovely mouth was stuffed with the just-budding breasts of the child, sliced from her body by the blood-thirsty machetes of the savage Negroes. Lastly, we found the sweet wife of don Rafael, but long we had to search in order to restore once again to its sacred wholeness the dismembered body which had been hers, hacked as it was to pieces by the merciless horde. Let it suffice to say that her breasts, now flaccid from her saintly years, and not so firm as those of the child Carmencita, were found in the family's silver soup tureen, and the head speared on the sharp top of a royal palm. Oh God! look upon the afflictions which mankind, still banished from Paradise, is able to provoke with such infinite wickedness and baseness. Those who read this, future witnesses of my relation!—strike from your souls any thought which extends to man the benefit of compassion! Awake! Open your eyes! Clutch not at illusions! Only mankind can stand against mankind!

Bishop Larra saw all his fears realized. The six months of uprisings, murder, desolation, and devastation that followed Baltasar's imprisonment made reinstatement a matter of utmost urgency. His return to power was the only hope for peace. Steps were immediately taken to free him and restore him to his post. In August 1768, Larra wrote the following letter to the Tribunal of the Holy Inquisition:

Beloved brothers in Christ:

It is with horror, as I cannot call it satisfaction, that my soul is stricken when I see fulfilled, as I had thought, the predictions and warnings which this day six months ago I communicated to yourselves with the intention of perfecting your understanding. The succession of revolts and rebellions which it has been our responsibility in part to meet, and which have embittered our understanding and our passions, will not be contained until the Crown's subject his Excellency don Baltasar Montañez is restored to the fullness of exercise of his authority in the office from which he was recently quitted. One must insist, however, that the civil authorities of this island not release said subject from his imprisonment until such time as the venerable authority of the Holy Tribunal, to whom this missive is addressed, lift those theological sanctions which, in the obscure and mysterious design of God our Father, have unchained these implacable Furies of hatred, vengeance, and destruction.

It is in virtue of the foregoing that I require of the high prudence and sanctity of this Most Holy Tribunal, a declaration that don Baltasar Montañez, subject of the king, is once more admitted within the pale of the Holy Roman and Catholic Church.

After six long months of bloody insurgency, Bishop

Larra won this round against the Inquisition's High Tribunal, for on August 24, 1786, the Tribunal set its seal to the following declaration:

> After a prolonged and most exacting examination of the causes which moved this Most Holy Tribunal to issue the finding of heterodoxy and willful, unrepentant, manifest, and obstinate heterodoxy against the person of his Excellency the Secretary of State of this island, don Baltasar Montañez, we find there to be most subtle theological arguments which alter, if not change altogether, our previous most sapient determinations. Under separate cover, in a volume of 10,000 quarto sheets setting forth the principle of motives,[13] we make known the painstaking theological road taken by this Tribunal in arriving at the determination that said subject Baltasar Montañez may once more be admitted within the pale of the Holy Roman and Catholic Church.
>
> With respect to the foregoing, we hereby declare that the aforesaid decision has in nowise been made for motives alien to the theological *corpus* pure and unsullied, and that from this determination no inference of

13. The Tribunal is here referring to a preliminary report of its reconsideration of the issues, a report totalling 10,000 quarto sheets, the equivalent of ten enormous bound volumes. The final reconsideration occupies three volumes of three hundred quartos each. This final reconsideration is what is known as "the principle of motives."

ignominious concession to any principle such as "reasons of state" should be taken, this principle, since its invention by the heretic Machiavelli, having brought fire and destruction, and eyes filled with hatred and spite, to every prince who has dared to invoke said doctrine, rather than Christ, as lighthouse and guide.

A smile must have passed across the features of Bishop Larra as he read this document. Under the "theological" justification not only of fear of constant mayhem but of the threat to the very existence of the white society, the High Tribunal of the Inquisition had acquiesced in the lifting of Baltasar's excommunication. But the subtle bishop's smugness could not have lasted long. During that same month of August 1768, a new and fearsome leader had arisen among the blacks in the northwest corner of the island. This Yambó had committed terrible atrocities among the plantations bordering on Lago Norte, leaving the ground behind him covered with cadavers and razed by fire and looting. And yet this new threat must have been the least of the bishop's worries, for still another stumbling block lay in the way of his plan for peace: Baltasar himself was now refusing to assume his former position. He would not be once again an instrument for putting down the insurrection—though not because of political conviction, let it be noted, or in solidarity with his black brothers. Instead, Baltasar had to all appearances quite simply gone mad. The hero had become a visionary, a zealot, a man possessed. The powerful of the earth had retreated into contemplation.

But was this latest renunciation on the part of Baltasar indeed the act of a madman who could not recognize the danger, the destruction, which his attitude surely entailed? Or had the cynical son of Ramón Montañez become the purest, most enlightened, and most wickedly evil of men? Those questions will be the subject of our next lecture, next Friday at the same time and in this same most hospitable place.

LECTURE III

In my last lecture, we viewed the desolate panorama of death and destruction brought on by the imprisonment of Baltasar Montañez. Tonight we will examine the mystery of that same Baltasar who, in renouncing power, perpetuated the slaughter.

By now it was a weary Bishop Larra who demanded Baltasar's collaboration in bringing about peace. On September 7, 1768, the bishop wrote him the following letter:

My dearest and most excellent friend—
It is with the humility which only the horror of so much bloodshed and destruction can inspire in this sinner, that I write, as on previous occasions, to supplicate you most feelingly to accept the full restitution of the powers which to yourself belong.

Since your refusal is implacable, and your heart deaf to the cries for compassion which ever before this day did move your noble understanding, the countryside of this island—which recalls the Paradise that God laid before our first parents—has been crossed with uncontainable rivers of blood, so that we cannot but contemplate the possibility that man is a beast, or the most savage angel of destruction. Only yourself, with the mien of moderation and peace which has ever marked your incumbency, can return humanity to these men who today strike not against the noble principles of Christian charity, but against the most elementary dictates of natural law.

On your shoulders rests the grave responsibility and moral obligation to bear—in tandem with the civil and ecclesiastical authorities of this island—the yoke of power, in order to avert all future and possible attempts on the public peace and common wealth of this realm; but it also lies within your power to exercise the force of your office of Secretary of State against those leaders of the sedition who may be shown to be enemies of humanity and a discredit to their race and people. You, sir, are the only man who is able to restore to its due place the noble condition of the race which now fills every innocent home in this island with mourning. I beg this action of you as a true hero to, and liberator of, the men and women of your people, a liberator who shall see how they may be led down the road of peace and obedience, who shall lift from them the burden of base passions and hatred which has provoked the most regrettable catastrophes to have blighted this island in many years. My hopes lie in your prudence and human compassion. For the good of all who obey the laws of human and divine society in this once sweet and peaceful tropical island of the Indies, may God enlighten your understanding!

What you have just heard is the *first* version of the letter

Bishop Larra wrote Baltasar. There are some changes in the final version, and in those changes we can see that the eminent prelate had certain reservations about what in fact the letter ought to say. In the final version, the bishop eliminated anything that he thought might be misinterpreted. The bishop had learned, or relearned, the lessons of prudence, and he was extremely cautious. He feared that Baltasar would react to his pleas for collaboration in just the opposite way. Expert psychologist that he was, Bishop Larra realized that any trace of condescension, reproach, or racial prejudice would send our hero even deeper into his madness. Therefore, in the following passage the bishop eliminated the word "obedience": "a liberator who shall see how they [*i.e.*, the Negroes] may be led down the road of peace and obedience," because he felt the word "obedience" would make Baltasar little more than the black overseer of the plantation. He also eliminated a passage that he thought might be seen as racist: "[a liberator] who will lift from them the burden of base passions and hatred." He threw out the end of that sentence too, because it sounded to his Jesuit ears like a veiled reproach: "...hatred which has provoked the most regrettable catastrophes to have blighted this island in many years."

But in the end, the bishop still failed. His task was an impossible one; the final version was no more acceptable than the first. And when he failed, he "lost it," as the saying goes, he was simply driven to distraction. He was now, though he probably did not realize it, a little mad himself. The cold, calculating bishop fell into a morass of conflicting passions. His fury at Baltasar's lack of compassion could not be concealed even by this most skillful of dissimulators.

Baltasar's reply to Larra, which I will read you in just a moment, is proof of our hero's progressive loss of sanity yet gain in lucidity. It is those two poles—insanity and lucidity—that sum up Baltasar Montañez' tragedy, for he was a visionary blinded by the light of his own vision; his tortured existence, he believed, was the path to a full understanding of the world. Here is that amazing letter:

To ask compassion of a man of truth is to make that man an accomplice in a lie which, like a warm and beautiful palace wherein men may forget the icy winds outside, has been built up, day by day, by guile and cunning, the opposite of mercy. I, the purest of men, the standard-bearer of truth, desire to see toppled all the cathedrals, all the lavish palaces that inspire men to forgetfulness. Thus it was that that good man of vision who taught me the magic of architecture and the disposition of nature by man's hand, taught me as well the path to our true condition, and on that path, his faithful loving disciple will follow him, to the happy music of many women and men, girls and boys, old women and old men—and Bishops.

Oh, what sweet architecture, faithful to that vision,

is mine! Out of the air I build, and I build with air; my desolate project, my ever-roofless palace, rises toward the silence and emptiness of the spheres. I am an artificer of the void, a nay sayer to the architecture and edifices which men have expressed and built for centuries. And therefore I offer, my beloved Bishop, the first and most fundamental lesson of the unsullied builder: Man, his back bowed and lacerated by the hard stone he carried, raised the edifice with the patience of the ant. Glory to God and the overwhelming necessity to forget that all that is built is a refuge against the empty heavens! Yet that hymn in stone, that burial mound wherein truth is entombed, was raised but the better to signal the emptiness: I see in the cathedral-palace an enormous finger pointing upward into the silent abyss of the sky. It is the magic of air; the more that space is filled, the more patent is the emptiness. How much remains before infinite space is filled! That emptiness is the promise of heaven; but once that hollowness becomes a lie employed by the most high and tragic superiors—and becomes a refuge for the many inferiors—it strikes me with terror, and I am sickened. Oh, how terrible is life whose face is turned toward the Void! All that men have pretended with their monuments is born but for the shroud. The monument is an uncreated act which dreams of God in order to deceive men. No more lies! Fiery subtleties spring from my cosmic plan! Creation devoured! . . . Yes, devoured by itself, I say, at the moment of its greatest definition. God created us from nothingness, because before his flawed attempt, nothingness did not exist. I would halt the deceitful compassion which destroys the truth that rises magnificent and naked into the air! And in that is my divine power, as the words of the master Juan Espinosa have foretold. Greatest power is that by which a man may cast men into the void. To deny them heaven is to correct the frail sentiments which God felt when He repented of the Creation. One must culminate the error, not correct it! For the eternal good of mankind! The greatest power is my renunciation of compassion. And as it happens, this renunciation is for the good of mankind. Compassion is the great double cruelty of a playful, repentant God. Let my breast not weaken! Onward with subtle reason!

Bishop Larra stood lost and without recourse before Baltasar's "subtle reason." In the letter I am about to read you, the now-pathetic bishop only begs, with rich sentimentality and poor judgment, that our hero help. His arguments suffer from every cliché of Christian piety, and beside the metaphysical profundity and originality of Baltasar's, sound nothing if not banal and pedestrian. This is the much-reduced bishop:

My dearest son—

You invoke reasons which oblige you to withhold from me your aid in the reestablishment of peace in this beloved island. For you, civil and ecclesiastical power, which in my person reside, is a prison for men, a prison built up from a succession of lies which for centuries have been necessary for the sweet community of mankind. But these lies, that good Christians call "white lies"—that is to say, lies which are merciful, pious, and good—are the sole warranty that man shall not become the most fearful beast. You renounce mercy, pretending thereby to reach the truth. You renounce my simple and true doctrines of Christ, yet thereby lose your soul in a theology without a God. Your ambition is divine, yet you are but little sensible to the pain which the many revolts and murderous attacks by outraged bands have brought to the ancient and desirable peace of innocent homes. For you, compassion originates in a God who repents His creation, repents a gratuitous act which became fierce cruelty. Yes, for in your theology life is more cruel than any martyrdom, as it originates in the clumsy error of a God who toyed with His powers. Yet in the last analysis of these most subtle arguments, we find old Lucifer, eternal nay sayer to Creation and to life: "Kill! Kill! Kill," he says, "with no restraint, and that will be the sweetest good to mankind—flee, turn yourselves from the face of Creation, which is universal stench!" Horrid, most horrid theology! The cathedral which your cruel purity (for sweet innocence it is not) raises over the purported ruins of a system of belief that gives mankind solace and shelter in this life, and the promise of another shelter to come, to fulfill the meaning of this—white truths, whose intention is to make man a creature of the Good.

But it is not within my spirit to give theological replies to your most cunning ingenuity; I only require that you have mercy, by the charity which in the spirit of Christianity your parents taught you, and that you set your eyes—which I imagine merciful—on the pain of the children mutilated in the continual slaughters, on the bodies piled high, the dismembered limbs, on the fields with their crops, the wealth of mankind, desolate now, burned by the destructive fury of those malcontents, those men who would strike at the divine plan itself. Make your own, that pain which fills the mothers who have lost fathers, mothers, husbands, children, and sisters and brothers, and cry, over this most desolate scene of carnage and death: Why? Why? Why, oh God, why?

Baltasar lost no time in replying to the bishop's unaccustomed, and melodramatic, sentimentality. His answer to the bishop's letter, a manifesto writ by patent genius,

speaks of a strange dream that symbolizes, or emblema-
tizes, the purity and heroism of his stance:

My dear, distraught Bishop—
To your clumsy, fragile arguments, I will reply with
only the indescribable beauty of a magnificent vision I
have had, a vision which is a sign above my head, the
emblem of my truths. It happened that fast asleep in
the depths where truth sometimes most cleverly hides,
I was given, by the occult nocturnal processes of my
singular spirit, a most magnificent vision, and this was
that vision:

　　There was a gigantic edifice, blind, as we say, in lack-
ing windows, and whose entrails were comprised solely
of stairways suspended in a huge hollow space and rising among the pyramidal walls like an interior universe
of stairways into the void. A design of confusion, which
symbolizes the most beautiful truths. And I ascended
those stairways, ascended within that high tumulus of
stone whose limits none for centuries had explored, not
even the fierce architects who built the prodigy. Stairways rising into the void, and all beneath the high
zenith which one could feel above! Oh roof unseen, but
which in thy ubiquity I sense! There thou art, more distant and unreachable than the precarious plans of men.
And I ascend toward thee, in order to know that void,
and then descend, and then ascend again, the distracted

journeys of the faith. But darkness and silence are thy accomplices, and under my feet I hear the crackling and rustling of abandoned plans, the hollow-sounding fall of a skull which shouts in infinite echo, the silent gaze of an architect devoured by his terrible madness. At this height, all is dead. I am now dragging myself up the steps which lead to the abyss, and my fingers touch my death before I hang suspended in that emptiness. Because at that, there is revealed to me my only sin, which is to remain suspended in the universal night. And so I drag myself down, and find new stairs which pull downward, an endless, fierce stepped ziggurat, toward the shadows where roofs may here and there be seen. Oh fever! Oh burning to culminate in something! Oh dream which with such terrible malice invites men to lose themselves in your infinite possibilities of ascent and descent! There, where not the slightest memory of sunlight remained, even the softest and most discreet farts resound with frightful universal echoes. All was noise in that silence, in that emptiness.

Then it was that there came, like a cataract falling upon my terror, the redeemers, the colossal crabs. It was the sound, nay the music, that would save us from the Creation. And thus it was that I realized how shameful my old aspirations and ambitions were, and thus it was that I decided to salute, from the dizzy height of my stairway, the marvelous antennae of those gigantic monsters. Their motives were benign, for soon they emerged into the sun, and began to lead the earth to its worldly limits, and I felt, under my happy feet, that the great edifice of the pyramid was giving way beneath me, and falling into the void, and a pleasure rose from my privates through my entire body, filling me with sweetest ecstasy.

Now the whole great pyramid was toppling; the world was devoured by the crabs, and it was then that the sweet sensation of falling possessed me. All was falling—crabs, pyramids, and men. Mankind now understood its past errors, and rushed to the benevolence of destruction. Oh Fall! Oh devoured globe of earth! Oh crabs floating in some corner of the universe!

Thus it was that the heart of humankind was much relieved. There was no more fear, for there was no down-pressing void. All Creation was devoured. There was no gigantic, fiery finger pointing. The most supreme act of liberation had been accomplished. Highest charity is forced, unrelenting, and gigantic destruction. And you speak to me of war, and the wide-spread slaughter that is committed outside these thick walls. Be aware that in my high plan, slaughter is sweet nostalgia, the true remembrance of those crabs who devour the Creation.

You speak, sir, of great and abominable crimes committed day after day, and which I alone can end.

But be aware that it is not my wish to avoid, forestall, or end them, yet on the contrary I am greatly pleased to see men launched upon the redeeming destruction of life. I know that those poor wretches act out their rebellion under the banner of my great name, and do so because I am for them the living image of their most hidden desires. I have had bread, while they have hardly tasted it; I have had power, while they can but dream of its sweet fruits. I do not deceive myself by thinking that my attraction is purely charismatic, magical, or in any great way theological, but rather insist, on the evidence of that which I hear, that the interest they maintain, in a ciphered way, in me, is for bread, which for this humble governor is a most noble matter yet for those wretches is heaven itself, and more, for they pass through life bearing their small domestic and civil tragedies—which are slavery, pain, and general silence.

So now I cry that I too rebel, like that one named Prometheus, and renounce all human desires and yearnings, and because of that, which is my renunciation of my frail humanity, I recover the lost motto of Luciferian mercy: Destroy! Destroy! Destroy!

I do acknowledge, sir, that my arguments are clouded by passion, but how else can it be, when I am driven to distraction by the things you have revealed to me. You say that unspeakable crimes have been

committed in my name, and that fills my heart with
wingèd emotion, for men agree with me. And now I
say to you that in their so-called "error" they show
their agreement with the Nature revealed to me as my
Garden, with my unique and blinding truth, which is a
vision for all eternity. For what subtle irony it is, that
they murder in the name of him who, locked within
these thick walls, is forbidden to do so. They are
angels! My angels of destruction! Some, the most ingenious of them, believe that they kill for justice. And
those pure ones are my most beloved brethren, for I
too stand before God with that grand word. They kill
in the conviction of the good they do when they
destroy life. Perhaps they think about *human* justice,
about *too much* human justice—but what is most
important, what is unique, is that they are in agreement with me, in words and deeds, if not in ultimate
motive. The sole concern, the most central concern, is
that for us, the Elect, blood is the greatest good. Some
may kill not out of ultimate motives, but for bread,
revenge, greed, and lust—the passions that all men
share. But I repeat that they too are my brothers, for
we are joined by the sweet agreement upon destruction. How lovely they are as they wave their bloody
machetes in the sun, and fall upon the tender flesh of
children! The man who kills is my brother, and even
the man who kills only on account of me shall be my

brother, even he who is the most wretched of all, for he loves without understanding.

There were once pleasant dwelling places in which those men known as the fortunate, or happy, lived. Their fields were arbored by olive trees, and crossed by the delicate streams of the Peloponnesus. The sky was a magnificent blue, and filled the souls of men and women with euphoria. The soft breath of flutes was heard throughout that countryside, and the hearts of men, who played games with naked children in the grass, were touched with grace. Cheerful was the bell of the bellwether when he came upon lovers clipping among the berry bushes. Oh! how sweet that place in which men lived in the air yet did not sense the terrible void. The peaceful blue sea of those isles was not water and only water, but the sea of the Greeks, the horizon of trade and poetry! There, upon those hills, there was no fleet fall glimpsed by the most impassive of glances. That dwelling place sheltered man. How distant were the cathedrals! And now I bring my arguments to a close, for I go to play fuck with the mighty *perico!*[1]

Bishop Larra's reply to the disconnected letter I have just read you turned impassioned in its own right. Con-

1. That is, he has put an end to the thoughts which obsess him, and is going to seek the euphoria brought on by the narcotic plant known as *perico,* which is the hemp of the nineteenth century, the *cannabis* of the twentieth, now extinct.

vinced that Baltasar was utterly mad, the bishop's
demands take on a tone of desperate supplication:

Dearest Secretary of State,
I write again to insist, your Excellency, upon the necessity that your will be put at the service of peace, and
that you once more exercise all those powers granted
you by virtue of your appointment. The endless murders which the rebellious bands continue to perform
on behalf of your restitution, which we have offered
you now countless times, have become unbearable to
the most elementary decency between humans. We
have word of the horrible slaughter of children. Two
days ago, in Fuente de Cocos, the dismembered bodies
of ten infants were discovered. And it is said that one
tiny creature had been carved into small pieces and the
pieces stuffed into the mouths of his little playmates. In
past attacks these blessed infants, martyrs to their faith,
had been sequestered on the prosperous plantations of
Villahermosa, Valle del Norte, and Sierra Chica. All
these horrid murders are perpetrated in your name,
and it is for that reason that I beg of the mercy innate
within you that you return to the office which alone
can put an end to this unbridled madness. For indeed
it is only you, and your most benevolent word, that can
pacify the violence which has been unleashed upon
our once peaceful island. And only you, I repeat, as the

most worthy representative of your race, can captain an
attempt to restore peace and tranquility to these
realms. Upon you depend the countless lives which are
today in grave danger. May God enlighten your mercy,
and recall you to your grave commitment to the welfare
of others which is implied in all offices of power!

On that same date, October 9, 1768, Bishop Larra
wrote the following in his diary:

What an effort it takes to thrust power upon those who
demand purity! This man who occupies my every
hour, my every hope and effort, parrots a great deal,
and one thing he says is that life seems to him an index
of the void, that he finds solace in the belief that terror
is the only mercy that can be shown the Creation. How
gross are his dangerous arguments! How far I feel
myself from him, I who have wielded power as a delicate compromise between compassion and terror! Yes,
for my hard life—since I can no longer pretend to
pleasant beatitude—is a delicate pendulum between
compassion, which obliges us to offer a dwelling place
for men, and the dark—how dark!—impulse to destroy
human life and all Creation. And seeking after the first,
I fall into the second, while in pursuing the second I
stumble out of necessity upon the first. Oh power, who
would have you! I am a slave to compassion and terror,

to the dwelling place in heaven held out to the bodies who no longer need it.

The bishop then adds:

I contemplate war and bloodshed, and I can attest that there is nothing in man that can serve as a lesson to mankind. Only a god, with his monumental, magnificent accessories, can keep men from seeing the nothingness reflected in the face of their neighbor, and, rendered zealots by the general innocence, or by young purity, from killing, killing, killing until all life is ended.

Here are two meditations by Alejandro Juliá Marín on the renunciation of our hero Baltasar Montañez:

THE HERO'S GLANCE

He sought an expression which would sum up his exhausting labor: Unrequited exercises in labyrinth building. Drawings that failed to achieve the precision of his dream. Cascades of paper sent to far-away apartments, from which no clear word returned. A model irremediably lost to his sight.

When his breath could achieve no more of such simulacra, he smoked a long pipe, which reinvigorated the attempt.

Accursed Nature was disposed so that we were

dragged down into it to our death. Under their masks of rational and geometric beauty, the avenues of acacias, the fences of royal palms and traveler's palms hid omnipresent and inexorable evil. This was his first assault on creation. It revealed the hidden curse of that which lives and grows.

THE STROLL

Each morning he goes out, to take the sun. He must be carried, with pomp and ceremony, up to the high battlements. Four strong Negroes bear the dolorous throne. Softly he brushes away the umbrella that would protect him from the sun's heat. The humble withdraw.

Out toward Pueblo Viejo and Laguna Alta, dense clouds of smoke are forming.

"Are they burning the squeezed-out cane?"

At last he discovered the only way. With no distress whatever, he stared into the sun. He forgot the light.

Bishop Larra was relentless in his determination to persuade Baltasar to collaborate. After the letter I read you a moment ago, the bishop made two more unsuccessful attempts. But this time his demands were not transmitted by letter; this time he "tempted" the hero's will with those pleasures attendant on power. Two visits to Baltasar's cell in El Morro prison were arranged. One consisted in taking six beautiful, and quite naked, damsels into the hero's presence; the other might be described as the presentation of the most exquisite delicacies of the bishop's table. Made desperate by Baltasar's constant refusals, the bishop thought he could bend the hero's will by appeals to man's most basic appetites: sex and food, or as the bishop's secretary put it, "sustenance" and "union with pleasant female beauty." These were the last assaults on the mystical seer's will power. Yet Baltasar remained unmoved in his renunciation of a power which would distort and betray the truth to which he had attained.

Bishop Larra's failure is chronicled in these two documents written by his private secretary, don Pedro Francisco de Zúñiga. Let me read you a part of them:

> As an act of extreme necessity of state, Bishop Larra determined to tempt the will of the subject Montañez with those two things which, as Aristotle has taught us, move all hard human labor, and these things are sustenance and union with pleasant female beauty.
>
> It was upon the twenty-fourth of October of the year of our Lord 1768 when a great crowd of the curious assembled before the Archbishop's Palace. The men and women there gathered followed, with hopefulness and prayers to the Holy Virgin, Bishop Larra's attempts to restore to his due power the only man believed able to bring peace once again between the races of this island, that man the subject don Baltasar Montañez.

The Infantry which accompanied the carriage of our kindly shepherd was obliged to fire into the air, in order to disperse the eager multitude which prevented the party from advancing. The object of the people's curiosity were six lovely damsels who were to be brought before the importuned yet unmoved Baltasar Montañez that very afternoon of hopefulness and prayers. Yet it was with great delay and commotion that the party at last emerged from the city, while once upon the field before the castle of El Morro it could travel more speedily, the carriage of our most beloved pastor and shepherd always protected by the courageous infantrymen of our most respected garrison. In the visage of our beloved pastor one might see the grave concerns of state which occupied his spirit throughout that march. And throughout the march, as well, one heard cries of *Bring forth Malumbi! Bring forth Malumbi!*

And once the party had arrived at the magnificent fortress, the Castle El Morro, trumpets were heard announcing the bishop, the ambassador of the royal will. The chief officer of our powerful fortress presented the keys of the garrison to Bishop Larra, who saw in person to the care of the beautiful ladies who were to serve as enticement and food to awaken the pity of our most beloved Lord Baltasar. How attentive the shepherd to the sweet ewes who would lure the strayed sheep back into the fold! As the bishop made the presentation of the

ladies to the Most Excellent Secretary of State, he exhib-
ited to the intransigent and demented prisoner the carnal
beauties of those females who inflamed every masculine
heart, and other pertinent parts as well. The females in
this showed a modesty that was a clear sign of their most
praiseworthy chastity. Yet the effect of this blushing
reserve was that our manly desires, so far from being
quenched by it, became still further inflamed. Many
wished to be that strange man who to our perplexity sat
looking out the bars of his window upon the furious sea
outside. He cast not one look upon those ineffable beauties, even from the corner of his eye. Yet what firm breasts!
what fleshy and inviting mounts! what lovely faces!

Yet that unfortunate, his mind absent upon what
errands God only knew, sat impassive both before the
graces of the damsels brought in to him and the reasonings of our shepherd. In all of us there present, there
sprang forth the most justified thought that this man
before us was not human in his passions, for with this disdain he could know not the satisfying of the most pleasant
appetite given mankind to enjoy. And our thoughts
seemed all the better founded when Bishop Larra
ordered the cell emptied, and, collapsing upon an arm-
chair there, his voice charged with most sincere emotion,
and tears about to mar his usually composed features,
said, "Baltasar! Baltasar! Why have you renounced your
humanity?" To which this hard, tempestuous, deranged,

and to all appearances unmanly (or unmanned) prisoner replied naught, save by the mad laugh that echoed throughout the stony cell.

Zúñiga's chronicle goes on to describe the second of the temptations, as well, which consisted, as I've noted, of the "delicacies of the table":

And more occasion was there to confirm the absence of human passion in that unfortunate, in the presentation to him of sweet delicacies of the table, invented by the cooks and dessert makers of our beloved bishop. A long file of servants marched toward El Morro Fortress, carrying trays freighted with the most precious treasures of the sea and of the land. In order that posterity may acknowledge the abundance of pleasures that our most prudent bishop lay at the feet of Baltasar, who was like a wolf, so surly and skittish he was, and so odd in all human comportment, I shall attempt to describe the comfits, roasts, pastries, and other things brought before him.

At the head of the procession went Bishop Larra, his great corpulence borne aloft under a canopy by four strong Negroes.[2] That afternoon was particularly

2. Documents and eyewitness accounts of the time confirm that Larra was extremely obese. Some claim that he weighed some hundred *levantes,* a unit of measurement that would put him at about three hundred pounds.

oppressive in its heat; but it was also most beautiful in
its light, which mingled harmoniously with the murmur of the waves of the Atlantic upon Sharks Point. It
was this heat which demanded that a huge Negro bearing fronds from that tree we call the traveler's palm—
for its fan seems to wave in greeting as the sailor nears
the shore —fanned our most Excellent pastor with cool
breezes, while the bishop himself sampled the cool col-
lations prepared by his private cook. This tonic-chord,
as it were, of cool degustation was followed by an enormous silver platter on which were pitchers of the fresh-
est nectars, and piles of all of the pulpy fruits which
grow on this blessèd tropical isle. There were
guanábanas, which are a type of *níspero,* and of the
same family as the tasty and most juicy custard apple,
or *corazón,* and *pomarrosa,* which is the apple of these
latitudes; enormous plantains were heaped up with
rich guavas and pungent pineapples like bulbous trea-
sure sacks of pure, rich, scented sugar. Behind the
delights of the tropical garden there came cornucopias
of the sea and the land. For me, the platter of seafood
held especial attraction—rich clams dressed with
lemon, whitefish and swordfish splashed with a red
sauce as piquant as it was savory, and with an abundance of onions, and the most wonderful salve for
these sore eyes, a lobster garnished with a sauce of
papaya. It was a labyrinth of subtle tastes out of which

one would never wish to find one's way. And I espied, besides, a plate of prawns as large as thumbs, and sauced with garlic and parsley. The crabs in their shells were as delightful to the eye as the taste of them was to the imagination, but this wonder was followed by conch, which is the meat of a seashell found about these coasts, swimming this time in vinegar and pure Spanish olive oil. After the treasures of the sea came those of the land, and first of all dishes of pork in every manner and variety imaginable. There were suckling pigs roasted to perfection, their flesh rendered crackling gold, blood sausages confected from the just-slaughtered sow, and fried and stewed tripe—the *cuajo* and *mondongo* of the island—and pigs' feet in rich sauce. But among the pork there was also jerked beef, shredded and stewed in a thick sauce of onion and tomato, and known among the populace by such colorful names as Old Clothes and Devil's Hindparts.

All this abundance was followed, before our feasting eyes, by thick stews of island tubercles—the *yautía, ñame, and batata*—combined with other tuberlike vegetables that grow upon our trees—the breadfruit, the bread nut, the green banana, and the plantain. In some of these stews there were also little balls of green plantain, grated and mixed with garlic or annatto—a delight to the palate, though not of pleasant appearance.

Almost at the end of this procession we came, with

our eager gazes, to the fowl—fowl stuffed with pickled eggs, with pimentos, with other rich stuffings of meat and other condiments, and with fruits of the sea. The true, and fitting, end was the dark coffee of the island, brewed in rich abundance.

The proof of the sweetness of these delicacies of the table is that the solitary prisoner was now in a better disposition to speak with the bishop, and soon even tasted the rich bait that the bishop had tempted him with. And most terribly disappointed were we who had accompanied the procession, for we had thought to sate ourselves on the leavings, believing the secretary of state would have none of it. But this time at least he contained his wild laughter, so that the servants brought up that whole train of rich delights to the ramparts of the upper part of the fortress, where the two eminent statesmen repaired for their meeting. There the tables were spread in glorious profusion, blessed by the good light, the sweet breezes, and the sight of the ocean's waves. And there the two men stayed a good while, savoring that carnival of flavors, while those of us in the procession remained below here, looking from afar at that odd *déjeuner sur l'herbe.* The matters discussed by the bishop and the secretary of state were grave, and the time for the discussion long. The hour of the lovely setting of the sun came, and the men's figures still could be seen, sitting or walking about the ramparts high above. Then night itself fell, and torches were lighted in order to illumine the deliberations that were taking place up above. I, my hopes for table scraps unfulfilled, went off to my own table at home, as I and my grumbling belly now began to long for my honored wife's humble fare.

Once again, Alejandro Juliá Marín has an insight into Baltasar's renunciation of even the most basic pleasures:

ALL IS ENDED

Baltasar became distracted once again. Toward dawn, the torches were extinguished. He returned to his stony retreat, and there he entertained himself by listening to the lamentations of the hungry that were scaling the inclined walls. There was the sound of harquebuses firing. Soldiers guarded that which tempted them.

The wonder of the world occupies the child. The old man's desires wane as death approaches. Only childhood and old age grasp the truth. Once one has tasted the light, pleasure has little to offer.

On November 8, 1768, three black men attempted to free Baltasar Montañez, a.k.a. Malumbi. According to testimonies of that time, under cover of a moonless night the three rebels approached the north wall of El Morro. They had reached the foot of the wall by crawling across the dangerous rocks of Sharks Point, where the fiercest surf of the entire coast batters the shoreline. There at the foot of the wall they remained in hiding all night. They were waiting for their hero's morning walk.

What I am about to read you is the report of what happened, a report written by Jaime Villaurrutia, secretary to the captain-general of the fortress:

Today, this eighth day of November of the year of Our Lord 1768, a most bloody event has occurred in the strongest bastion of all this Caribbean Sea, by which I mean our most beloved fortress San Felipe del Morro. Three malign and seditious Negroes have attempted to abduct our Most Excellent Secretary of State Baltasar Montañez. And this fit of madness has been undertaken here where don Baltasar resides in community and honor, in the most strong and excellent fortress San Felipe del Morro. Forthwith I shall relate how this shocking attempt occurred: After crossing the rock-encrusted shore of Sharks Point, one imagines with great risk to their savage lives, the rebels climbed up to the lower battlement on the north face, and there they waited until the dawn, when don Baltasar came out upon the ramparts for his daily walk, for I repeat that it was their intention to capture and steal him, and even to demand a high ransom of the civil authorities of this island. But they erred in their pretended horrors, for it was don Baltasar himself, whom they intended to steal away, which sounded the alarm, and this is the way this part occurred: The rebels made signs to don Baltasar, signalling that he should approach the battlement, so that, hidden by the shadow of the wall, the three of them might escape with him. It was at that moment that don Baltasar called out to the soldiers who protect his person, and do so with the strictest vigilance from the higher battlement. But it chanced that the guards did not hear don Baltasar's cries for help, and I report this in accordance with testimony given before the captain-general. The wicked Negroes then attempted to drag our Secretary of State away by force, as force was the sole recourse to which their base reason led them. To judge by the statements of the guards on the battlement above, it was at this pass that the cries of don Baltasar grew loud and vociferous, for the guards have stated that at first, when they did not hear them, the cries were very weak and faded, but that afterward, when the madmen attempted to drag him away by force, don Baltasar cried out in a loud and piercing voice, and those were the alarms that woke the entire garrison, whose soldiery then put to rest the pretensions of the vile abductors.

But that is to anticipate the end, and so I return to the matter: There came a moment in which the three rebels seized our beloved Secretary of State, and would not allow him his freedom. But God, whose special care it is to protect the welfare of our authorities, granted great and miraculous strength to don Baltasar, who in escaping from the pretended abduction left the rebels helpless, for they were now without their hostage, and exposed to the marksmanship of our artillery. Thus it was that the abductors were wounded, and finally killed, by a fierce fusillade of cannon and harquebus, so frightful that every man of their cursed race would have fled in fear had they been present. But I have not stated that at the moment of the first firing, only two were killed, and that later the other attempted to flee, but fell to his death on the knifelike rocks of Sharks Point below. And as all know, the name of this place derives from its sharp-edged and most toothlike rocks, which jut up like the teeth in a shark's mouth from the coast, and in this I do not exaggerate. There was, thank God, no wound or harm done our most beloved Secretary of State, and proof of this is that he lost neither his composure nor his consciousness, but indeed paternally calming his guard, and brushing aside all the urgings of the garrison's authorities that he retire to his quarters to rest, he continued his walk, as though nothing had occurred.

Bishop Larra wrote in his diary about this event, and even showed some sympathy for the black rebels who

were attempting—like Larra himself—to bring Baltasar
back into a position of power. Let me read you an excerpt
from this part of the bishop's diary:

This afternoon I visited the site of the attempted abduction of don Baltasar Montañez, and as I looked upon
that blood, still fresh, that lay upon the pavement, a
throng of painful thoughts assailed my spirit. Most
brotherly I felt toward those who had left their blood,
and their hopes, spilled there. They, like I, were victims
of the hardness and pitilessness of this man. Their
dreams cried out for a hero, a liberator, a satanic man
able to lead them to the alteration of the order decreed
from time immemorial by God. Yet it is not in the causes
of these occurrences, but in their effects—not in the
motivations, but in the events—that the great wickedness
of mankind is seen, for when one thinks of it, these men
want a thing which is called Good, without qualifica-
tion, but which in its train, in its immediate effects,
brings the most horrible pain to this beloved island.
How soon good strays from its true path! But I confess
that they did wish great good for their race and their
people, and that this harsh, pitiless man has exacted
from them and their ambitions a terrible price in blood.
Yet I am brother to them, and that, because I too am a
victim of his renounced and most accursèd power. I
believed that this man was the sweet compromise

between the races of this lovely isle. I have failed, with a din that shakes the universe, and have done so because he has turned this fair tropical land into a scorched and bloody wilderness. Yet my passion was good, as was the passion of those men who left their blood here. And I must accept that I am the brother of these men in their most human dreams and yearnings. All these things I thought as I stood before the wide pool of blood, and then I sensed something which disturbed my person. I looked up, and there he stood, upon the highest battlement, that blasted and accursed man who had won that struggle with the men who now at last obeyed the cruelty of his vision. There I saw him, as though some simulacrum of God, and my soul leapt back in revulsion.

Oh you poor wretches! Brothers in the suffering of this most inhuman cause!

As we might have expected, Alejandro Juliá Marín has given us a meditation on this attempted "liberation":

THE SUICIDE

They collided with the truth, and its gaze made their souls sink. Their dreams heard a volley of red explosions that their surprise could not grasp. From euphoria to emptiness, like the soldier who, raising a flag on the captured peak of a hill, hears suddenly an absurd whizzing sound. . . .

One remained, though he still did not understand—the one who brought his forefinger to his lips just as his muscles turned old, wise, desperate. They say he tried to get away, but I say that colliding with the truth is a serious matter.

The following dialogue, excerpted from another of Juliá Marín's plays, *The Hero's Renunciation,* imagines that far-off conversation between the bishop and Baltasar Montañez, up there on the battlements of San Felipe del Morro. Oh, the power of the poet, the writer of possible history!

BISHOP LARRA: Can you not have considered the cruelty implied by your vision? Do you not realize that this truth of yours is no good for living? Only the white lie makes community, society, living one with another possible; without the white lie, humanity is not the limit of man.

BALTASAR: Don't be cynical. Man is a rational animal; community, society, living one with another is based on reason, as is man's instinct for self-preservation. That is why man need not be subject to a lie.

BISHOP LARRA: The clear sightedness, the freedom from illusions which allows me to see mankind's wickedness and evil, you call cynicism. Baltasar, Baltasar! Do you not see that stupidity is more powerful than the instinct of self-preservation? I have been a confessor for many, many years, and I tell you that man is the only animal who in doing harm to another harms himself. That is his grandeur and his tragedy. In that, man is angel, but also the most fearsome of beasts. And as for "reason"... On that head I have nothing to say.

BALTASAR: In deforming and distorting mankind, power justifies its own existence. Your pessimism makes man an eternal slave.

BISHOP LARRA: *(Indignant.)* How dare you speak of slavery! Do you not see that your renunciation has unleashed the bloodiest uprising in the history of our island? You have unchained the beast that lies inside men. That reason, that rationality which you make so much of, is the slave of hatred.... Your "freedom" murders children....

BALTASAR: *(Interrupting.)* Don't try to play on my emotions. Those miserable creatures rebel for reasons that have nothing to do with me. Of course with their slaughter they do collaborate in the destruction of all creation, which is supreme freedom.

BISHOP LARRA: You do not know what you want. You trust in reason and the instinct of self-preservation, but then you delight in a freedom which destroys that which exists.

BALTASAR: *(With irony.)* "That is his grandeur and his tragedy!"

BISHOP LARRA: Who is the cynic?

BALTASAR: I trust in mankind's ability to survive without God. But I also trust that man, in an act of supreme freedom, will prefer to destroy, to destroy everything. And thus we will have corrected God's greatest error—creation....

BISHOP LARRA: *(Indignant.)* A madman, a suicide, and a self-contradictory one! You renounce God, but not rebelling against Him. You renounce the divine, but you still believe that the creation is a "divine error." That confirms what I have always thought— all cruelty is the twin of belief.

BALTASAR: *(Fallen into deep introspection.)* You do not understand me. It is belief in your horrible God that burns at my entrails.

BISHOP LARRA: All right, all right ... Enough of this twisted theology. I have come to ask that you take up the reins of government. It is the only means of bringing about peace. Day by day more children die, men and women are sacrificed to the cry of *¡Viva Baltasar! ¡Viva Malumbi! (Sarcastically.)* Very well, I also cry *¡Viva Malumbi!* ... I beseech you to assume the responsibility which circumstances have forced upon you. It is upon your conscience.

BALTASAR: *(Still sunk in introspection.)* Speak not of my conscience. The death of innocent people is a relief to me, the relief of seeing creation gutter, little by little.

BISHOP LARRA: *(Enraged.)* You are perverse. You climb to Olympus, and once upon its peak you refuse to speak the white lie which makes life possible. Your cruelty has no limits. Accursèd man!

BALTASAR: *(Turning sarcastic.)* My dear bishop ... The white lie has always existed, but so have wars. Man is the only animal who feels repugnance for creation. And that repugnance is more powerful than all white lies together.

BISHOP LARRA: *(Half to himself.)* If he is this way cool, how must he be in heat?

BALTASAR: *(Smiling.)* Pleased!

BISHOP LARRA: *(Very solemnly.)* Please, let us not return to subtleties. Your people need you, your race needs you, and so does and do mine. We are all the victims of your renunciation. For the last time, I beseech you to accept the power that is yours.

BALTASAR: *(Cynically.)* What powerful theology!

BISHOP LARRA: *(Visibly distraught.)* You are a monster.

BALTASAR: *(Quietly, as though half to himself.)* I renounce God and mankind, two faces of the same error.

BISHOP LARRA: *(His voice weak.)* You are a dangerous monster. . . . The only consolation that remains is that mutations such as yours occur once every thousand years. . . .